DR

'Sorry to disrupt the f
seemed an appropriate moment. I've just come from the bank.'

'I see. What's the prognosis?'

'In the short term, superficially at least, Drummonds is sound enough, but infirmity is bound to set in sooner or later. There's no capital, George, and it doesn't take an expert to see that unless we form a strategy for rebuilding, we will be in serious trouble . . .'

'We have a bank loan.'

Sir Foster looked down at his glass, but didn't drink.

'They won't go on with it, old chap.'

George leaned across the desk on his knuckles, his face thrust forward, his eyes fixed on Sir Foster, in unconscious imitation of an attitude he employed to convey absolute authority to miscreant boys.

'The school will survive.'

DRUMMONDS

William Gilmour

ARROW BOOKS

Arrow Books Limited
17-21 Conway Street, London W1P 6JD

An imprint of the Hutchinson Publishing Group

London Melbourne Sydney Auckland
Johannesburg and agencies throughout
the world

First published in Great Britain 1985

Set in A.M. Bembo by Photobooks (Bristol) Ltd

Printed and bound in Great Britain by
Anchor Brendon Limited, Tiptree, Essex

ISBN 0 09 943760 0

1

Drummonds was not built to accommodate so many cars, and they were parked wherever space would permit, those belonging to the parents of older boys familiar with the territory nosed boldly between the buildings, while the main driveway was lined with those that had brought the babies, as the school's new boys were customarily known. This name, spoken affectionately by the staff whose concern was their care, but sneeringly by senior boys, seemed especially appropriate on the September afternoon that marked the end of the summer holidays and the start of the autumn term, since several new arrivals were in tears, uncomforted either by fatherly assurances or the squeeze of a mother's gloved hand, as their footsteps faltered on the yellow gravel.

Few took in the school's pleasant proportions, its warm red brick façade, green lawns and playing fields surrounded by great chestnut trees already prickly with the conkers they would battle with before long. They saw instead a grim prison where they would serve a sentence for no other crime than being eight years old and the sons of parents able to afford eighty guineas a term for their education. Far from feeling privileged, they felt unwanted and more numbingly alone than on any other day in their life. They were told that they would learn to love Drummonds, and the cries and laughter which accompanied the preliminary rounds of ragging between older boys were offered as proof of their future happiness, but those sounds only served to intensify their sense of isolation.

'Look at the little blighters – they've not the remotest idea what they're in for,' Christopher Fordham remarked, as he rocked on his heels by the window, his back turned to the common room, his observation addressed to himself as much as his colleagues. 'In their oversized blazers and squeaky shoes, sending desperate messages to mummy with every tearful glance and tightening of the fingers, as if even in this eleventh hour she might somehow be persuaded that her little ray of sunshine would be better off at home.'

'So cynical so soon, Christopher?' murmured Patrick Heritage, looking up from the untidy pages of *The Sporting Life* and pushing a shock of thick white hair away from his forehead.

Fordham half turned to answer the older man.

'What else can they be thinking? About the imminent delights of Latin declensions and algebraic equations that you and I will share with them? I think not. Those are as yet unimagined pleasures. Any hot tips today?' he inquired, indicating with a nod the columns of runners and riders on Heritage's lap.

'I'd have had a flutter with Siggy, were he here. I wonder where the good doctor is.'

Heritage stood up, stuffing the paper between the seat cushion and the arm, and joined Fordham by the window, where he stared briefly at the scene outside before jerking himself abruptly away.

'Seen it more times than I care to remember,' he grumbled wearily. 'Same faces, same uniforms, different names, that's all, and a lot of them turn up again a generation later. When I was your age, it was a sight that filled me with hope. I felt I was helping mould men who might make the world a better place to live, but too many of them ended up as names on the school's roll of honour to keep that hope alive – and the country's in another awful mess right now,' he added unhappily.

'And you were suggesting I was cynical, Patrick?'

Fordham peered along the narrow bridge of his nose at Heritage, who shrugged.

'I'm a realist, no more, no less. All we can do is pass on the little that we know.' He returned to the window and waved a hand testily towards the boys struggling with trunks and tuckboxes. 'What they make of that knowledge is something we cannot control.' His finger fixed on one unmistakable newcomer standing awkwardly beside the row of parked cars on the drive. 'Take that boy. We have him until he's thirteen, and that's all. Still,' he sighed, 'let's see what we can do.'

Fordham followed the pointing finger and studied the boy, who was now approaching the school, hand in hand with his mother. 'I'll tell you one thing,' he said, 'I wouldn't care to risk half a crown on which of those two is closer to tears.'

Had Mary Prior been able to hear that remark, it would certainly have set her off before her son, for the short walk to the school's front steps was the most agonizing exercise so far in a day whose painful progress had begun with the packing of Edward's unfamiliar new clothes into her own favourite suitcase, and had been punctuated by a series of rituals whose normally mundane nature had been replaced with a devastating sense of finality: his last bath, his last meal at home, the last straightening of his tie and combing of his hair. The drive, through scenery she normally found uplifting, had been almost unbearably miserable, the long silences during which she could feel her son's resentment surging from the passenger seat, where he had been allowed to sit as a special treat, interrupted by her inadequate attempts at optimism. And now Drummonds itself.

'The headmaster wants to say hullo to us both, Edward, and then you'll be able to meet the other boys. I'm sure you'll like them.'

As if reminded by that remark of the function of the building he was about to enter, Edward stopped on the steps and tugged his mother's hand hard enough to prevent her progress towards the door at their summit.

'I don't want to meet any other boys. I don't want to meet the headmaster. I want to go home with you.'

'Darling, we're going to be late.'

'Mummy, please.'

'Edward, you promised me you'd be brave. And you liked Mr Drummond when you met him before. Don't make us late.'

Edward bowed his head, but allowed himself to be led through the open doorway and into a large hall which had been empty when they had visited the school before, but now throbbed with the movement and noise of boys and their parents. He shuffled close to his mother's side as she hesitated at the edge of the crowd.

'Mrs Prior? And Edward?'

Edward responded to the inquiry by raising his eyes from the polished floor and saw a smile that penetrated even his resolute defences, reinforced by an encouraging squeeze from his mother's hand before she withdrew it. She too was taken with the smile of the crisply uniformed young woman in front of her.

'How d'you do? I'm sorry we're so late.'

'Not at all – better late than never.'

'We're supposed to be having tea with the headmaster.'

'Which is precisely why I've come to lead you through the throng. All the other new parents are in the headmaster's study. Shall we lead the way, Edward?'

Edward glanced nervously at his mother as an unfamiliar hand took his and began to propel him briskly between the stares of other boys, but she answered with a reassuring smile to which she added a nod of delighted acknowledgement as their guide announced over her shoulder, 'I'm Wendy, by the way, the assistant matron.'

The route to the headmaster's study was as short as it was straightforward, but Edward's senses were sufficiently confused by his new surroundings that he would have been hard put to it to retrace his steps had an opportunity for escape presented itself. As they entered the room he had an impression of bookcases, of framed photographs of young men in uniform, and of a dark, imposing desk which was partly obscured by people with teacups clutched to their chests who all looked to him a good deal older than his mother and who turned when Wendy announced their names. Several men who were sitting down stood up, and Edward observed the smiles they showed his mother resentfully. While the adults in the room looked at her, the boys who, like Edward, were about to be abandoned offered him no more than a hopeless collective stare. He wished he was beside his mother, to hold her hand if he could, or at least to touch her, to breathe her familiar scent, but Wendy was between them, an impassable starched white wall.

The headmaster's voice redirected each uncomfortable stare and Edward recognized Mr Drummond by his grey hair and by the bags under his eyes which gave his face an unhappy look except when he smiled, and reminded Edward a little of a dog. He heard Mr Drummond say how nice it was of him and his mother to join them, and then his mother apologized for being late, which caused him to look at the floor in case anyone eyed him accusingly. He was counting worn threads in the carpet so intently that he missed the first words of welcome, but managed to harness his attention as the headmaster began to address the new boys, and he listened, half fearful that some grim ritual might be ordered, half hopeful of a last-minute reprieve. As it was, he heard neither.

'You boys might be wondering what's happening to you today,' George Drummond said with a smile that was meant to reassure. 'Starting at boarding school is a big event in anyone's life. But we're a family here, a home from home, and there's a great deal more to school than the lessons you'll learn in the classroom. School should also be a place where we all learn to live with each other and care for each other, and school should also be fun. So never hesitate to ask if you have a question, to laugh if you find life funny, or to say so if you feel sad.'

Edward was trying to absorb these ideas and was considering telling the headmaster that he was already feeling very sad indeed when the talk took an unexpectedly practical and instantly unsettling turn.

'Now,' said the headmaster, in a tone that was no less pleasantly paternal than before, and yet chillingly final, 'if you would like to follow matron, she will show you to your dormitory.'

Edward barely had time to shoot a look of panic at his equally anguished mother, before Wendy whisked him into the corridor along with the other new boys and began to herd them at once towards a broad staircase. When he looked back the door to the headmaster's study had closed between him and his mother, and though he glanced over his shoulder several more times he knew because his heart was heavy that she would not come out and that he was alone now. His eyes prickled, but he knew he must not cry.

His desperate sense of solitude was made more acute by the very air that hung about each passage they penetrated on their way to the dormitory. The intermingled aromas of perfume and cigar smoke in the headmaster's study had not been unlike those that pervaded his own home on occasion, but the strange smells which Edward now began to distinguish were altogether less familiar. From one doorway, which he identified later that afternoon as the dining room, came an odour that crept into his nostrils and caught uncomfortably at the back of his throat, and which, even after being traced to its source in the kitchen, he found hard to associate with the preparation of any dish he was ever served; the stairwell, where the arrogant eyes of older boys had to be avoided during the ascent, gave off a mixture of floorwax and disinfectant; and the landing with its adjacent laundry room had a starchy freshness which reminded him at once of his grandmother's house and waiting by the airing-cupboard door to be wrapped in a warm white bath towel. But as Edward's nose adjusted to the smell of carbolic from a nearby bathroom, which quickly overpowered that of clean linen as they filed along the corridor after Wendy, his senses were distracted by the sight of a figure approaching from the opposite direction.

*

Charles Drummond in turn observed the pitiful procession at the heels of the assistant matron and noted a quickening of Wendy's steps before she turned into the baby dorm, which left the boys adrift. He arrived at the doorway as they did.

'So you're the new arrivals, are you?' he asked cheerfully, but the boys were either too shy or shell-shocked by the events of the day to answer. 'Wendy's showing you your dorm, is she?' He went on, 'Well, come on, let's all have a look together.' And he wrapped an arm around the shoulders of the last in the hesitant line and followed the boys into their dormitory.

The dormitory was warm and lit by the afternoon sun, which threw bright diagonal bands across the red rugs that covered the four beds by the windowed wall. The four beds opposite were in shadow, but otherwise identical, iron-framed and narrow, their covers tucked in so tight it looked impossible for even the slightest boy to slip inside without first loosening them. Beneath each bed was a white chamber pot, and beside each bed a wooden chair and a faded tan rug; the floorboards were otherwise uncovered. There was no other furniture and few fittings: grey curtains whose folds had become striped by sunlight, radiators like squat, cast-iron concertinas, an engraved illustration of a Bible story, and a row of pegs beside the door.

Anticipating the boys' reaction to the austerity of the strange room in which they would have to go to bed that night, Charles was quick with a suggestion he had heard his father make in the same circumstances. 'If you've got teddy bears in your cases they'll be up soon, so you can unpack them and put them by your pillow. And don't worry, you won't be the only ones.' He allowed that scrap of comfort to be absorbed, before continuing. 'My name's Drummond, the same as my father. He's George and I'm Charles, but I'm afraid you'll have to get used to calling us both "sir", as you will the rest of the masters. I may not look much older than some of your big brothers, but that's the way it is. And what are your names?' He looked inquiringly at Edward.

'Edward – sir.'

'Well, Edward, that's a problem, because I know there are several other boys in the school called Edward, and I need to know which Edward is which, so what we do at Drummonds is call every boy by his surname. So what's yours, Edward?'

'Prior – sir.'

'That's much better. No other Priors here, are there, Wendy?'

The assistant matron, who was plumping a pillow busily, glanced up and shook her head.

'And that's another thing you'll need to learn,' Charles added. 'I just called Miss Ferguson Wendy, but you won't. You'll call her "Miss Ferguson", always. School rules – you'll get used to them. Now I must go and say hullo to your parents, but we'll be meeting again on the football field, if not before. I hope your boots are all properly dubbined.'

Several boys, Edward among them, looked puzzled. Charles grinned.

'I think you've taken in enough for the time being,' he said. 'Dubbin will have to wait.'

As he made to leave, Wendy told the boys, 'Find your beds. I'll just be a moment.' She tapped the rail at the foot of the bed by the door. 'They've all got a name on.'

Outside in the corridor she grabbed Charles' sleeve.

'Have I done something wrong?' he asked, his buoyant tone deflated.

Wendy glared at him.

'I want to talk to you.'

'Why?'

'I have to talk to you. Please?'

'What about?'

'Something important, which concerns you, Charles. I may have to leave the school. But I can't tell you here . . . now.'

The urgency of these last two whispered words was justified by a desperate cry behind her.

'Matron!'

Charles checked Wendy as she twisted away from him to identify the voice.

'Why on earth?'

'Please,' Wendy hissed. 'Come to my room tonight. I'll be off duty about ten.'

Before Charles could answer a breathless boy arrived, and he spoke to him instead, adding an admonishing edge to the voice he had used in the dormitory.

'Don't run.'

'I wasn't running, sir,' the boy protested.

'And don't contradict,' Charles added severely. 'Why the mad panic to see matron anyway?'

'My mother's forgotten to pack any vests or pants, sir. What am I going to wear?'

The boy's eyes turned anxiously to Wendy, but she said impatiently, 'You're not supposed to be unpacking yet.'

'But my tuck's in my trunk, sir,' the boy whined.

'That's not an excuse,' Charles said, but added encouragingly, 'however I'm sure Wendy will see what she can do for you.'

He looked at her for confirmation of this promise, gave a muttered assurance that he would see her later in her room, and hurried off along the corridor in the direction from which Wendy had brought the boys.

*

If cups of tea alone could have convinced the new boys' parents that their sons would be well looked after at Drummonds, there would have been no need for its headmaster to answer a stream of questions that sprang from the same source: parental concern for a child who now, as the moment of absolute separation approached, seemed too small and too vulnerable and too young to leave on his own. Eventually every area of school life had been explained and approved, though not before every mother had had to endure the image of her son being bent over a bath and beaten, a form of discipline, George was quick to point out, very few boys brought upon themselves.

'I take full responsibility for your children,' he reaffirmed for the eighth time. 'The staff and the school, we are the essence of England – God, Country, Drummonds.' He allowed a slight smile to qualify his hyperbole, and returned to mundane matters. 'Boys get a clean shirt every three days and we are great believers in fresh fruit. Ah, Charles – ' He interrupted himself, as the door opened, and announced proudly, 'My son.'

'How do you do?' Charles' greeting was more formal than his accompanying smile. 'I've just left your offspring happily inspecting their dormitory.'

'Are they settling in all right?' Mrs Prior asked.

Charles' smile sparkled in his eyes.

'Oh yes. A bit bemused, perhaps, but that's to be expected.'

'Charles?' His father's voice contained a mixture of command and entreaty which diverted his attention from Mrs Prior. 'I wonder if you would show Mr Brown around the school grounds. He hasn't had the opportunity to see them.'

A hand, thrust towards Charles, singled out Mr Brown from the others in the room, as, sartorially, did the yellow windowpanes woven garishly into his brown suit. The large, squarish hand and the strength of its grip as Charles shook it, had a physicality unusual amongst Drummonds parents, and this aspect of his presence was emphasized still further when he stopped at the top of the stone steps the moment he emerged from the building and drew a deep breath, as if his system had been deprived inside of an essential supply of fresh air. Sensing an explanation was required, he slapped the parapet of the shallow portico.

'Bricks and mortar, that's my game. Solid, see, like me. I'm not a great one for words, coming out with them or listening to them, but I know my business. And I know what's best for my boy, which is why I'm prepared to fork out nearly ninety quid a term to get him a better start than I had. So what are you going to show me first?'

'Would you like to see the football pitches?'

'I can see they're green and flat enough from here. What about the drains?'

'The drains?' Charles repeated doubtfully.

'If the guttering and downpipes are anything to go by, they're probably in a pretty ropy old state. No offence meant, but the place looks as if it could do with a few bob spending on it.'

'Albert, you will offend the young gentleman if you keep on.'

Mrs Brown's intervention had indeed prevented Charles protesting at this attack on Drummonds.

'Don't get me wrong,' Brown went on with a conciliatory gesture, 'I'm not saying it's falling down, and the decoration's all in good nick, but it's not always what you can see that causes problems. And like I said, I know building. See? Can't leave the job even when I take a day off. Maybe you'd better show me those soccer pitches after all, otherwise I won't get a moment's peace on the way home.' Brown winked at Charles, while Mrs Brown frowned at her husband. 'That's the one trouble with a Rolls, the engine's so quiet you can hear every word.'

Charles grinned despite himself, and began to outline the school's educational standards as they strolled across the grass, but Brown cut him short.

'You needn't bother – your father said it all. Impressive man.' Charles nodded in agreement, as Brown continued, 'And I'd heard enough about the school already to know Paul's come to the right place. Each to his own. I can turn a pile of bricks into a handsome house, but I'll leave it to you to turn my boy into a sharp young man. You won't catch me interfering with the way you run the school.'

He surveyed the green expanses, newly lined in white with goalposts gleaming in the sunlight, and dug his heel into the turf with evident appreciation. Then he turned back to view the school itself, shading his eyes from the sun.

'Drummonds is a fine place,' he said after some consideration. 'But don't forget what I said.'

'It is,' agreed Charles. 'And I shan't.'

Unused perhaps to standing still, Brown shuffled his feet and shook his arms in the manner of an athlete limbering up, an unexpected flurry of movement, which his stocky frame and loud suit made even more unlikely. He stopped as suddenly as he had started, and ran a finger inside the neck of his shirt.

'Can't be doing with a collar and tie on a day like this,' he declared loudly, then, ignoring another disapproving frown from his wife, tugged his cuff away from a gold wristwatch. 'We ought to be getting back, dear. Better say goodbye to Paul.'

'Yes, I can see some of the parents leaving,' said Charles helpfully. 'I think I might be needed. If you don't mind making your own way back. Mrs Brown. Mr Brown.'

Charles' hand tingled slightly from the pressure of Brown's parting grip as he set off at right angles towards the drive. The line of cars was no longer continuous, the sleek profiles of those still parked in twos and threes forming a meaningless word in morse code. Charles could make out Mary Prior and Edward, and tried to guess which model hers might be so that he would arrive as they did. He was only a few yards away when they suddenly stopped, and he lengthened his stride as he saw the boy throw himself against his mother and bury his face in her jacket. He heard Edward moan, 'Don't go, Mummy. Please don't leave me here.'

Before Mrs Prior returned the desperate embrace, Charles gently prised the boy away from his mother.

'Come on, Edward. Let's go inside. You've only seen the inside of the headmaster's study and your dorm. There are lots more interesting places than those. I'll show you.'

Edward sobbed silently, but turned towards the school, away from his mother. Mrs Prior reached hesitantly for the car door handle, without turning it.

'Edward'll be all right,' Charles said confidently. 'Won't you, Prior?'

Edward looked up, blinking back tears.

'Yes, sir.'

The boy hardly heard his mother's murmured goodbye as Charles propelled him towards the school entrance, pointing out landmarks as they went, while searching for a more durable topic of conversation.

'Ah,' he exclaimed. 'Here's Brown saying goodbye to his parents. Have you had a chance to get to know him yet?'

'He's in the next bed, sir.'

'Well, I'm sure you'll be firm friends before you know it. Come on, I expect he'll be pleased to see you.'

Mr Brown stopped drumming his fingers softly on the roof of his Rolls-Royce and spoke to his wife.

'Here's young Mr Drummond, dear. He'll sort it out.'

Mrs Brown looked relieved.

'Oh yes. You talk to Mr Drummond, Paul. We've got to be getting along.'

The Browns climbed into their car; Charles put a hand on Paul's shoulder.

'What's the problem, Brown?'

'She took my white mouse.'

'Well, I'm sure he'll be happier at home – and you'll still be able to see him in the holidays.'

'Not my mum – the one in the bedroom. *She* took it.'

'I think you'd better start again, Brown. And do try to remember. I'm sir, your bedroom's a dormitory, and *she* is Miss Ferguson. You'll get the hang of it.'

'Miss Ferguson took my pet mouse, sir. It was in my pocket. I put it on the bed. Miss Ferguson said he'd have to go in a cage, sir.'

'And what does he live in at home?'

'A cage, sir – but a nice one. And he's happy at home.'

'Let's get you settled in first, Brown. Then we can see about your mouse.'

During the course of this conversation Charles had succeeded in spiriting both boys back to the building.

His father was standing on the steps, and pronounced their names as they passed.

'Brown. And Prior. You see? We're friends already.'

Charles pushed them gently into the hall.

'You'd better see to your unpacking now.'

He waited for their answering chorus, then joined his father.

'Watching the parents depart?'

'I was,' George answered irritably, 'until a moment ago. Since when I've been watching the chairman of the board of governors arrive – unannounced.'

A Rover rolled gently to a standstill on the gravelled sweep in front of the school.

'What does Sir Foster want?'

'Damn it! The first day of term. Why on earth does he have to turn up today? Look, Charles, would you do me a favour?'

'You mean another one?'

'I'm sorry, Charles, yes, you've been marvellous already. Other things on my mind. But would you mind dropping into the common room and making sure the new man gets introduced to everyone. Paint him in a good light. You know the sort of thing.' He moved to welcome the military-looking man who was marching with stiff briskness towards him, but checked himself momentarily. 'By the way, you must tell me later what you made of our Mr Brown.'

Sir Foster Gill mounted the steps at a slight sideways angle.

'A word, George,' he said with no other greeting. 'In my study?'

'By all means.'

The two men did not speak again until George had closed his study door behind them.

'I take it this is a matter of some urgency, Foster.'

'Sorry to disrupt the first day of term, George, but it seemed an appropriate moment. I've just come from the bank.'

'I see.'

George gestured tentatively at a decanter on the bookcase.

'Can we still afford sherry?'

Sir Foster gave a gruff laugh.

'Good Lord, I hope things never get that bad. Pour away, George.'

George filled two glasses, an operation which Sir Foster observed with a critical eye.

'Economizing already, eh?'

George gave the decanter another nudge, so one of the glasses was almost full to the rim, and offered this to Sir Foster.

'Good health, George.'

'My health has never been better, Foster. It's the health of the school that concerns me. What's the prognosis?'

'In the short term, superficially at least, Drummonds is sound enough, but infirmity is bound to set in sooner or later. There's no capital, George, and it doesn't take an expert to see that unless we repair, unless we maintain, unless we form a strategy for rebuilding, we will be in very serious trouble. When Her Majesty's Inspectors come in next year and see the decrepit state of the roof, let alone the wheezy plumbing, the dicky central heating, the dry rot –'

'We have a bank loan.'

Sir Foster looked down at his glass, but didn't drink.

'They won't go on with it, old chap.'

He watched George slowly lower his glass to the table, where he left it.

'I'm sorry. You're an old friend, George, and much

loved. And a darn good influence on the younger generation – building character, preserving the independence of young minds, young heads, young hearts. And that's bloody important, because this country's in need of new ideas and new spirit.' He punctuated his speech with a sip of sherry. 'But that's me speaking. Not the voice of the bank. The bank is saying, "The coffers are empty." And if the coffers are empty, Drummonds will go under.'

'I don't believe it.'

'You must, old chap.'

'This school is the heart of many people's lives – it's loved and admired. My life is dedicated to it.' He strode behind his desk as if to take stock of his study from a more accustomed viewpoint; he looked at the faces framed on the walls, remembering names and voices. 'Drummonds belongs to every boy who's ever been here. It belongs to the staff, to the boys they'll teach this year, and next year, and the year after. It represents their future. Our future. The school cannot close.'

'Then you're going to have to come up with an idea. Or rather, I suggest you're going to have to find a fairy godmother – except I don't believe in fairies.' Sir Foster drained the last of his sherry and twirled the stem of the glass between his fingers. 'Believe me, George, I'm as devastated as you are by the news. A way of life is ending.'

George leaned across the desk on his knuckles, his face thrust forward, his eyes fixed on Sir Foster, in unconscious imitation of an attitude he employed to convey absolute authority to miscreant boys.

'The school will survive.'

'I sincerely hope it does.' Sir Foster rose, bringing an air of conclusion to the topic. 'By the way, how's our new appointment?'

George started at this change of tack, and for an instant seemed to struggle for the name.

'Binny. I asked Charles to ensure he meets all his colleagues.'

'Hope the school takes to him. The man's something of an OLLC. One of life's little curiosities,' he added in answer to George's arched eyebrow. 'But he is a friend of mine.'

Commander Tim Binny had not made the task of introducing him easy for Charles. He had grimaced pointedly at the rumpled pages on Heritage's lap and bristled at the cat curled on the school secretary's, unimpressed by Miss Fisher's assurance that the animal was an institution; he had belittled Fordham's achievement, or so Christopher considered, of having scored with book and pencil, not bat, for Glamorgan; dismissed Dr Gunz as a boffin; and pulled rank on Major Bertie Braithwaite, the school bursar. Only Susan Pusey had come through the formality quite unruffled, owing partly to a common interest in art, but more perhaps to a dark, if rather severe, beauty which Binny found disturbingly attractive, and to her tact.

Oblivious of the impression he had made, he now stood in the centre of the men's common room and announced himself.

'I'm a naval man and a Christian. My aim is to get chaps thinking hard – damn hard – about the Church as a career.' He hesitated and made a sudden humming sound which refocused the wandering attention of his colleagues, before he spoke again. 'And sex!'

Now every eye in the room was on him, causing his cheeks to redden.

'Do I understand that you wish the boys to consider

sex as a career?' Fordham asked with an exaggerated concern which hinted that he hoped to get the better of Binny, while one corner of his mouth threatened to sabotage his straight face.

An abbreviated hum preceded Binny's answer.

'Of course not, man. I want to talk about sex.'

'Really?' Heritage encouraged him to continue.

'To the boys – sex in the context of the Church.' He wheeled on Charles. 'I must talk to your father about delivering a sermon.'

Charles cleared his throat uneasily. 'Yes, well, I'm not sure what my father's plans are on that front just yet.'

'Or in the classroom. I shall be prepared to talk about sex to the school whenever duty calls – with care, calmness and complete frankness.'

'And diagrams, Commander Binny?' Gunz inquired.

Binny ignored the question, addressing Charles instead. 'Sex is a serious subject – more serious certainly than my fellow masters would have us believe. I shall take the matter up with the headmaster.'

'That's probably the best thing.' Charles smiled cautiously. 'Anyway, we're very pleased to have you.'

The silence that seconded that statement was broken by Miss Fisher.

'Do have a cup of coffee, Commander Binny.' She poured as she spoke and thrust a cup at him. 'And come and sit with me and Susan. After all, we're here in your honour – we're not normally invited into the men's common room, you know.'

While Binny was cornered with coffee and biscuits, Charles joined Fordham and Gunz, who were elbow to elbow by the cluttered mantelpiece.

'A conspiracy?'

'The man is totally dire,' Fordham muttered.

'Dreary, pompous and opinionated. I fear Moral Rearmament is in our midst.'

'Somc sort of nervous trouble,' Gunz suggested. 'Inferiority complex.'

'Don't judge him too soon,' Charles pleaded. 'Let's see if we can make it work – somehow.'

Uncertain as to the degree of optimism with which he could honestly endow an account of Binny's introduction to the rest of the teaching staff, Charles was anxious to direct conversation away from the unrest in the men's common room as he dined with his father that evening, but indirectly brought the subject up himself.

'What did old Gill want?'

His father bisected a slice of meat with a precise stroke of his knife.

'Nothing much. Checking up on Binny. What do you think of him?'

Charles had expected a longer answer, and his mouth was full. He chewed thoughtfully for some moments.

'Rather grim and gloomy. Altogether a bit of a square peg.'

'Well, I want you to do everything you can to make sure his appointment works. For his sake, for the school's sake, and because the chairman of the board of governors is supporting him.'

'Is that really the only reason he came? A personal interest in his protégé?'

'He advised me to remarry – for the good of the school.'

'And what did you tell him?'

His father's smile had the effect of a shrug.

'If the right woman were to come along, then perhaps.'

'So now it's Binny and marriage broking. Come off it, father, there must have been something more.'

'Nothing you need worry about, Charles. Only money, as ever. Nothing changes. All we need is some capital.'

George's tone carried less conviction than his words, and Charles set his knife and fork untidily on his plate.

'If the school's short of cash, why not ask that chap Brown? He's made of money.'

'But not exactly the sort of chap we want charity from.'

'Why not? He's a highly successful building contractor and he's also very aware that we need money. Do you know, he has a rather endearing enthusiasm for drains.'

'I'm more concerned about Binny than Mr Brown.'

'Binny's one thing, father, money's another – whether you like where it comes from or not. And Brown's right, the drains are awful.'

'I must say,' said George distractedly, as if Charles had not spoken, 'I thought Mrs Prior was most pleasant. A ravishing smile. Very pretty indeed.'

'I agree.'

Charles lifted a tankard from the table and studied his father's face above the brim while he drank.

'I believe she lost her husband in some ghastly motoring accident. He was a captain in the Marines. Awful tragedy. Fortunately his family have private means. They insisted on the boy coming to preparatory school, though I suspect she wasn't too keen. She lives quite near, you know.'

'So she picked the nearest one?'

'Mmmm. Not exactly the most flattering of motives, is it?'

Outside, the school clock struck a half hour. George checked his watch, picking up his napkin in the same movement, which he then folded, rolled and slipped inside a silver ring, before placing it carefully on the polished surface of the table, an inch to the left of his empty plate. Charles recognized the ritual.

'Off to say goodnight to your babies?'

'They'll be missing their own beds. I like to think it makes a difference if I put my head round the door.'

'I'm sure it does.'

'Coming over?'

'I thought I'd pop over later. Look in on the senior dorm. See who's telling tall stories after lights out.'

Wendy sat on the very edge of a bed just like the boys', her hands on her knees, and her fingers crossed in case some crisis should call her from her room before Charles came. She tried to identify the patterns of approaching footsteps, heard the headmaster's slow stroll and Fordham's, or so she guessed, confident clicking stride, and then quick, light steps which stopped outside her door. The room was so small she could have opened the door from where she sat, but she felt too nervous to be still, and was on her feet, the handle already turning in her hand, as two soft taps confirmed a visitor.

Charles was in such a hurry to get out of the deserted corridor where, even under the subdued night lights, he was conspicuous for a dozen yards in either direction, that he pinned Wendy against the wall as he pushed the door open. Once inside he backed against the window, taking care not to disturb the curtains.

'I think I've got a bottle of beer somewhere,' Wendy said with forced steadiness, and at once produced a bottle, glass and opener from the bedside cupboard. The top popped as it came off and the neck of the bottle clinked against the glass as she rushed to control the flow of liquid. More footsteps came quickly along the corridor, causing Charles to stiffen, a finger pressed urgently against his lips, but they continued past Wendy's door.

'I can't stay long. I've got to do my rounds.'

Wendy handed him the glass, wiping its base with a finger.

'Sorry about the froth. And do sit down. You make me nervous.'

Charles remained by the window.

'So what's so vital, Wendy?'

'I've something important to tell you, Charles. Look at me, please.' She waited for his eyes. 'Have you no idea what it is I want to say to you?'

'I hope it's pleasant,' Charles said as brightly as he could.

'I love you, Charles.'

Charles' steady gaze wavered, but he saw Wendy shudder.

'If you're going to behave so distantly towards me – I'm going to have to give in my notice.'

'Isn't that a bit strange? If you say you love me? I think you can't if you'd consider leaving.' He took her hand. 'You're not to give in your notice, please.'

Wendy chewed her lip.

'I do love you. I wouldn't have let you make love to me if I didn't.'

'Yes.' A pause. 'I'm sorry.'

Wendy's eyes flashed at the apology.

'Sorry? How can you say that?'

'I am sorry,' Charles repeated uneasily. 'It was just – I couldn't help it.'

'Is that all you can say?' Wendy demanded angrily. 'You said you loved me, Charles. "Sorry" – that's a terrible thing to say. You couldn't *help* it – that's cruel, incredibly cruel.' She had taken her hand away from his, but in the silence that followed her outburst she reached for him again. 'I adore you, Charles. You're all I want.' She tugged his hand to emphasize each word, like a parent driving home a lesson to a child. 'Charles, marry me, please.'

'What could I offer you?' he asked, adding his own answer quickly. 'Nothing. You're very sweet, Wendy, and I'm very fond of you –'

'Fond!' Wendy interrupted bitterly. 'That awful word – the one that means "I don't love you". But I love you, Charles, I love you very much.'

'It's not that, Wendy. How could I marry you? Where would we live? I wish I could say yes, but I can't.' His voice dropped a tone. 'I'm not the type.'

She felt him strain against her hold, realized she was gripping him more tightly than she meant, and loosened her fingers.

'Please, Charles, if you can't say yes now, don't say no. You might change your mind.'

'Fine. But I must dash.'

Charles made for the door, rubbing the back of his hand. Wendy dropped on to the bed and fell back against the pillow; as she stared unseeing at the shadowy rectangle of ceiling, her tears traced glistening lines to her ears.

Long after lights out, long after the comforting chatter had been silenced by the dormitory prefect with a warning that the head would be back with his cane, long even after the last loud sobs had given way to sleep, Edward Prior and Paul Brown still whispered across the space between their beds.

'I wish I knew where my mouse was – I'd go and get him.'

In the darkness Edward was wide-eyed at Paul's bravado.

'It's rotten of them to lock him up all on his own. I hope the cat can't get him.'

'What's it called?'

'Whitey.'

'No, the cat.'

'Paddy. He's going to be my friend.'

'Are you going to be my friend?'

'Yes.'

'Do you miss your mummy?'

'A bit. I wouldn't if I had Whitey. Do you miss yours?'

'Yes.' Edward hugged his teddy tighter. 'Why didn't you say your prayers?'

'I don't have to at home. Did you say yours?'

'Yes.'

'What did you say?'

'God bless Mummy and let her come to see me soon.'

'Do you live a long way away?'

'I don't know.'

'I live in London.'

'Is that far?'

'I think so.'

'Are you tired?'

'No. I'm allowed to stay up late at home. My parents let me watch television. Have you got one?'

'No.'

'Why not?'

'I don't know.'

The sound of feet in the corridor evoked in Edward a

vivid image of Mr Drummond, a cane held high above his head, and he jerked his head under the covers, his eyes clamped shut and his teeth clenched as if flinching from a blow. Paul, however, faced the door defiantly, and Charles could see the boy's eyes were open.

'Is that you, Brown? Go to sleep. You'll be exhausted in the morning.'

Edward's heart was still pounding when the footsteps faded, and he dared not move.

'Are you asleep, Prior?'

'No.'

'Why are you hiding?'

Edward brought his eyes level with the fold of the sheet.

'I'm not. Who was that?'

'Mr Drummond – the young one.'

'He's nice.'

'He won't let me have Whitey back.'

'I'm tired,' Edward said, afraid to risk further conversation.

'I'm not.'

'I'm going to sleep.'

'I'm not.'

Paul half propped himself up on his pillow, a position which surprised Wendy when she came to wake the sleeping dorm next morning.

2

'Can't stand to see those miserable suburbs coming,' Sir Foster Gill announced by way of explanation, as he settled into a seat with his back to the engine. 'You can warn me of their approach, George, and I shall concentrate on the crossword until we touch the buffers in Victoria – unless I finish it first.'

George Drummond looked round the first-class compartment which they alone occupied.

'In our current financial crisis I can't help feeling we ought to travel third class.'

Gill snorted indignantly.

'If you want to travel with the other ranks, you're welcome. But pinch or no pinch I go first class – which reminds me, don't let me forget to present you with a petty cash chitty for my ticket.'

'No, Foster,' George answered drily.

Gill studied the accelerating scene outside until the view was suddenly shortened to the steep chalky bank of a cutting, and he turned to face George with a satisfied smile.

'Charles is to be congratulated on two counts, then.'

'Sir Foster?'

'It was he who suggested you try this chap Brown for a donation, wasn't it?'

'Yes, it was, and I'm afraid I rather pooh-poohed the

idea at first. One doesn't like to admit it, but that reaction was nothing more than good old-fashioned English snobbery – like you and your first-class travel.'

'Absolutely, old boy, but when it comes to cash, the money all smells the same. Apparently the man's a millionaire. Probably got rich erecting those awful estates which seem to creep further into the countryside every time I come to London. Better make it clear we don't want any jerry-building at Drummonds.'

'He hasn't offered to help us yet.'

'He will, if I know anything about his sort. He wanted money and he's got that. Now he wants something more. Substance, status, call it what you like – that's what we can offer him in return for his cash. And I'm sure our Mr Brown will regard a hefty hand-out as a small price to pay for that. You'll see.'

'If he doesn't, there's always prayer,' George said. 'But you said Charles was to be congratulated on two counts?'

'Yes, I'm surprised you didn't bring it up yourself, George.' Gill's teasing smile narrowed as George stared blankly back. 'Don't tell me you don't know?'

'Sorry, Foster. I'm completely in the dark.'

'You mean Charles hasn't told you he's getting engaged?'

The pullman's wheels rattled uninterrupted across several sets of rails before George recovered sufficiently from the news to shape his scattered thoughts into a question.

'You mean to the assistant matron? To Wendy?'

'I'm sorry to spring it on you, George. It seemed fairly safe to assume Charles would've told his father. Had you no inkling?'

'He hasn't said a word.'

'Well, perhaps you'd better not let on it was I who told you. The boy must have his reasons for keeping mum. Seems odd to me though, I must say.'

'How did you get to hear about it?'

'The girl told her uncle – and Judge Deacon, as governor, evidently felt he ought to inform his chairman.'

'When?'

'The other day – when I spoke to him about our meeting with Brown. And I hardly think he'd be one to talk injudiciously – if you'll pardon the pun. Really, George, this is most embarrassing. It's not as if I'm the bearer of bad tidings. Wendy strikes me as a delightful girl.'

'I agree. It's a bit of a surprise, that's all.'

'Frankly, I think it's rather a good thing. I've said it before, George, the school needs more married men on the staff. If Charles marries, you could consider giving him greater responsibility. He's young, but I think he would make a splendid deputy head. And in the long term . . . who knows? A married couple – really, George, I can't tell you what a difference it makes to prospective parents.'

'As you say, Foster,' George murmured, 'as you say.'

On one wall of the ante-room of Albert Brown's inner office was a scale model of a new town development mounted like a bas-relief of the cubist period. George hoped Gill would not notice it, or if he did, would not pass comment. Luckily, in the few moments they were made to wait, Gill was too occupied with Brown's private secretary, specifically with the portions of her thighs which could be viewed via the kneehole of her desk, which led him to compliment Brown misleadingly on her helpfulness as soon as they were shown into his sanctum.

'Yes, indeed, general. Marvellous girl,' Brown agreed. 'Don't know what I'd do without her. Tea, gentlemen? Coffee? The real thing,' he added with a confident wink.

George declined gratefully, but Gill requested a cup of tea. 'If it's not too much trouble to make it for one.'

'Nothing's too much trouble for you, General Gill. I was a sergeant-major in the Middlesex all the way with you to the Rhine.'

Brown's face shone with pride.

'Splendid, Brown. Damn good regiment.'

'People get it wrong about the war – great days they were. Off you go, Ronnie. One tea for General Gill.' He waited for the door to close behind his secretary's swaying hips, then said eagerly, 'Now what can I do for you gentlemen?'

Gill looked at George, indicating that he should speak.

'When you visited Drummonds, you commented on the condition of the school buildings. The drains.'

'And the rest, Mr Drummond.'

'Exactly.' George cleared his throat. 'We are in very real difficulties. The fabric of the house is in poor repair and we need capital investment.'

'Use the bank – that's my motto. That's what they're there for.'

'We have, Mr Brown, but they haven't given us all the support they might have.'

'I've got a lot of confidence in banks. You need confidence.'

'Good show,' said Gill. 'That's what's made you a very successful man.'

Brown leaned back in his chair and savoured the general's praise.

'I like to think so,' he agreed. 'And that's what I want young Paul to have – confidence and character – the sort of things I never learned till I joined the army.'

He looked from Gill to George, who asked, 'Can you help us? Financially?'

'I always believe in coming straight to the point,' Brown said approvingly. 'I put my money where my mouth is. Usually I put my mouth where the money is, if you'll pardon the expression.' He hesitated, before adding firmly, 'I'd want to see the books.'

'I'm certain we could arrange that,' said George, encouraging a nod of confirmation from the chairman.

'I'm a serious man,' explained Brown. 'I care for the future. Ours is a great country and we didn't fight for it so as a load of Attlee types – Bevan, Bevin, Dustpan, Dustbin – could tell me what to do with my money. I'm a traditional man, cautious, conservative. It takes someone like me who didn't have a penny once upon a time to want to hang on to what he earns. I want to help keep this country great. I never had the luck to have a smart education, I'm not the sort that gets into the MCC or a gentleman's club in Pall Mall, but that doesn't mean I can't help people of a different class, just because I don't talk the way they do.' He looked from one face to the other across the desk. 'I'll be blunt, gentlemen. What I want is a memorial for my mother, before the old girl turns up her toes.'

'A memorial?' asked George.

'A building – something special. We'll get someone in from the Royal Institute of British Architects to design it,' said Brown, enthusiastically. 'We'll make it a British endeavour.'

He caught a look between George and Gill.

'I know my station, but I also know I could be of use to you. So I'll pop down and have a look at the books – and look the place over properly while I'm at it. Any day suit you, Mr Drummond?'

'As long as you telephone first to make sure I'm available.'

'Give you time to cook the books, eh?'

Gill coughed.

'Only joking, General.' Brown turned to George. 'And don't say anything to the boy, Mr Drummond. Let's make it a surprise. See how he's settling in.'

Paul Brown, like the other new boys at Drummonds, was adapting rapidly, if reluctantly, to the routines and rituals of school life. He could pleat his bedclothes into hospital corners, stand shoulder to shoulder unabashed at the urinal, traverse every corridor and staircase, mumble 'Amo, amas, amat,' but more importantly cry 'Ego!' in answer to 'Quis?' and 'Bags I' or 'Fains', as the occasion demanded. But, unlike the other new boys, Brown burned with a feeling of injustice that was more powerful, more permanent than even the ache of homesickness that inhabited every bed in the baby dorm after lights out.

Eventually he tracked down his white mouse in the biology room, crouched in a cage on a cluttered cupboard top. Whitey, he felt sure, looked unhappy and ill-fed, and he returned to the room during mid-morning break with some crumbs from his currant bun. He was almost caught when Dr Gunz burst in, but the science master was only intent on a pile of exercise books and missed the barely hidden boy. Alone again, he opened the door of the cage and felt in his blazer pocket for the food, but the sight of Whitey sniffing excitedly between the bars stopped him, and he reached instead inside the cage, scooped up his pet and slipped it inside the pocket which contained the crumbs. Uncertain how long he could rely on the supply of food to keep the mouse from moving, he cupped his hand carefully inside the pocket, a position that caused his arm to stick out awkwardly and consequently attracted the attention of Mr Fordham as boy and master closed on each other in the corridor.

'Something in your pocket, Brown?' Fordham asked. 'I think you'd better let me have a look, don't you?'

Brown produced his pet reluctantly and looked imploringly at the master.

'What are you doing with that revolting creature?' Fordham said with exaggerated horror, ignoring the look. 'You'd better give it to me at once, and get out of my sight before I decide to report this serious breach of school rules to the headmaster.'

Brown placed the mouse on the outstretched palm and watched Fordham's fingers curl around it.

'Don't hurt him.'

'Brown, your concern for our dumb friends is most impressive. Didn't I catch you trying to feed the school cat at tea yesterday?'

'Yes, sir.'

'Well, I shall expect this interest in animals to reveal itself in good biology marks. I shall ask Dr Gunz to let me know how you get on. Now, get along. You can have your rodent back at the end of term.'

The end of term was an unimaginable age away and Brown brooded over his imprisoned pet. The longer he pictured it alone in a cage in that room full of strange smells, the angrier and unhappier he became. Had he confided his feelings to a member of staff, as the headmaster had encouraged every new boy to do on that very first afternoon of term, he would have found more than one sympathetic ear and, what's more, having sounded an emotional alarm, would have been placed under unobtrusive, but constant observation. As it was, his sudden disappearance before scripture was unforeseen, while Binny's enthusiasm for his subject delayed discovery still further.

'The Bible is my book,' he assured the boys staring dumbly from their desks. 'I read it every day. Millions do and so should you. People throughout the world take comfort from its words – and such exciting words they are!' For a second he was distracted from his theme by a poorly disguised yawn. 'Tired?' he asked the boy, but went on without waiting for an answer. 'When tired, consider the Sermon on the Mount. I want to convince every single one of you of the importance of this book.' His eyes darted from face to face as he continued. 'In this era of Socialism, we rightly have a union – a scripture union. Our dues are belief! Belief. Write down this thought for today.'

Binny's confident gaze suddenly clouded.

'Are we missing someone?'

Prior put up a hand.

'Brown, sir.'

'Mmm' – Binny's involuntary hum, indeed 'a binny', as the master's vocal tic had already become known to Drummonds' bigger boys, announced oncoming anxiety – 'does any boy know where he might be?'

An answering silence prompted a louder, longer hum, before Binny spoke sharply. 'You boys had better look at your Bibles. Study the Sermon on the Mount. I'd better see what's happened to Brown.' An upsurge of excited whispers behind his back made Binny turn at the door. 'The Bible is best read in silence,' he boomed with a warning wave of a finger.

In the men's common room Binny alerted Charles and Bertie Braithwaite to Brown's absence. The pair made immediately for the headmaster's study.

'Bad news,' Charles blurted to explain their intrusion. 'Paul Brown has apparently disappeared.'

George stood up from his desk at once.

'Are you absolutely sure?'

Charles answered with a sketchy shrug. 'As sure as sure can be.'

'When?'

'He's supposed to be in Binny's lesson. He isn't. No one's seen him since break.'

George looked at his watch.

'Well, he can't have got far. He's bound to be here somewhere. I'd certainly rather like to find him, wouldn't you?'

Ten minutes later the school had been scoured and the search extended as far as the school gates.

'We've never lost a boy in our history,' George said a trifle breathlessly. 'And this boy of all boys – on the day his parents are due to visit us.'

'Binny must have scared him,' Braithwaite muttered.

George looked from him to his son.

'Agree, Charles?'

'I don't know. I would've thought there'd be more to it than that.'

'Did he seem odd? Unhappy or anything?'

'Not that anyone's mentioned. Do you want me to ring the parents?'

'Not yet – not until we've made a complete search.'

'Police?' suggested Braithwaite.

George shook his head emphatically.

'I would have thought if he was going anywhere, he'd be trying to find his way home,' said Charles.

'Then take the car and go down to the village,'

George urged. 'Check the bus stops and ask at the station.' He watched Charles run towards the school, then looked urgently at Braithwaite. 'Is there anywhere we haven't looked? Dear God in heaven, we must get him back.' He thumped his palm with his fist. 'Why did it have to be Brown?'

After slipping cautiously past the classroom windows, Brown had sprinted the length of the drive, fully expecting to hear an angry shout behind him at any moment. But he reached the gates unpursued and crouched in the hedge while he got his breath back, all the while keeping one eye on the school and the other on the deserted road, and at the same time trying desperately to remember from which direction his father had driven up to the school entrance. When he had recovered sufficiently and opted, without a great deal of conviction, for one way rather than the other, he began to walk briskly beside the verge, looking back repeatedly. At length a car appeared in front of him and slowed as it approached. Through the windscreen he could see the driver wave, but the man's lop-sided grin made him feel uncomfortable, and as the car braked to a stop he panicked and bolted through a gap in the hedge behind him. He glanced over his shoulder as he ran, and the sight of the stationary car caused him to run even faster, his speed and the rough ground almost tripping him several times before he plunged into a thicket where he slowed, partly because he was now entirely out of sight of the road, partly because of the density of the undergrowth, and partly because he was quite exhausted. He walked on, panting, towards the sunlight at the other end of the trees, and eventually emerged into a field; he slumped to his knees, aware only that his heart and his head were pounding furiously, but before he could relax, he was catapulted into another bout of panic by the wheezing clatter of an ancient tractor exploding into life no more than twenty feet from where he knelt. The boy stood up, but could summon neither thought nor strength to make another move.

Seeing him, the tractor driver turned off his engine and called down from his seat, 'What are you up to, young man? You lost?'

'No,' Paul said shakily.

'Where are you off to then?'

The tractor driver swung a leg and clambered down. Brown made a break across the open ground, but was quickly overtaken.

'You won't get anywhere running over there,' the man advised kindly.

'Please, I want to go to London,' said Paul, suddenly on the edge of tears.

'London, is it?' asked the man. 'Aren't you from the school?'

'Yes.'

'Why would you want to be going to London, then?'

'I'm going home.'

'I see,' said the man, with a friendly pat on the shoulder. 'I suppose you'll be wanting a lift, then?'

'Yes, please, sir,' Paul said excitedly.

'Ever ridden on a tractor before?'

'No, never.'

Paul's eyes shone with delight at the prospect of a lift home on a tractor, but he became less confident a few minutes later when, after bouncing along a rutted track perched high on the driver's knee, they emerged on to the road. The view was disconcertingly familiar.

'Are you sure this is the way to London?'

'You'll see, young man,' the driver assured him, then pressed the engine into a deafening roar.

Even on the metalled surface the tractor rattled enough to keep Paul's knuckles white where he could find a hand hold, but the tautness in his body caused by clinging on dissolved sickeningly at the sight of the school entrance. He would have jumped, had he not been hurtling along so far above the road and been barred from the grassy bank beside it by a solid left arm and leg. He looked accusingly into the driver's eyes, which were watery from the wind; the man's gaze did not waver from the road as he spoke.

'This is the only home I'm taking you to.'

The tractor's tyres sprayed gravel against the bars of the open gate, as it turned into the drive almost without slowing, and peppered the grass and flowerbeds on either side with small stones, eliciting an angry look from a gardener who was deadheading late roses. The sight of this unlikely vehicle also brought George to his study window, and a moment later had him hurrying for the door, leaving Charles enlightened only by his exclamation: 'I don't believe it!'

Paul sat sullenly on the steps, stroking the school cat and watching the tractor driver point across the playing fields, his arm stretched towards the distance. The boy's dejected state seemed to impair his hearing, because he could not concentrate on the explanation or the questions and answers which drifted vaguely at the very edge of his attention. His view of the school gates was uninterrupted and he saw a car materialize between them, noting absently that it was a Rolls-Royce of the same shape and shade as his father's, but it was Charles' voice that penetrated his mood.

'It's Brown! He's here already.'

Paul stood up, puzzled; Paddy rubbed against his

shins. Aware of the nearness of the boy, Charles spoke close to his father's ear. 'You don't need to tell them. They probably won't find out from Paul – he'll just make a joke of it. You really don't need to say anything, father. Let it be.'

George gestured that he would greet the Browns alone and walked to their car. The three of them stood in conversation for some minutes before the headmaster called Paul's name and he joined them apprehensively.

'I'll leave you to it,' George said. 'Might I suggest a walk in the grounds? You can find your way to my study, can't you?'

'Certainly, Mr Drummond. Thanks very much,' Brown answered, with less bluster than usual.

He and Mrs Brown walked either side of Paul.

'Why, son? Why did you do it?'

'Are you unhappy, dear?'

'Course I'm unhappy – they took my mouse.'

Relief from the tensions of his escapade, suppressed until his parents' worried inquiries, now released a flood of tears. Mrs Brown rummaged in her bag for a handkerchief, while her husband glanced quickly over his shoulder, cleared his throat, and said, 'Come on, son. Don't want anyone to catch you crying, do we?' Mrs Brown dabbed Paul's face with a scented square which bore the crimson impression of her lips.

'There's plenty more mice in the world,' Brown advised.

'But Whitey's *my* mouse. And everyone keeps telling me what to do. When I've got to go to sleep. What I've got to eat. I don't like it.'

'You mean it isn't like home.'

'No, it isn't.' Paul looked at his father. 'It's like prison.'

'Nonsense, son,' Brown said sharply, but softened his

tone to continue. 'Now you just listen to your dad. If you go back in there and stay put, I'll see to it that you get a whole family of white mice.'

'Albert!' remonstrated Mrs Brown.

'And a new cage?' asked Paul.

'And a new cage. Now go on – get stuck in. Don't let your mum and dad down.'

Mrs Brown bent to kiss her son and give his face a final wipe with a licked corner of her handkerchief, and blew her own nose as the boy ran towards the school.

'I cannot disguise the fact that we have let you down,' George said, pacing the gap between his desk and the window. 'And I shall perfectly well understand if you wish to turn down our request without further discussion.'

'What request's that?' asked Mrs Brown.

With a remarkably delicate gesture for so substantial a man, Brown leaned from his chair and laid his fingertips on the back of his wife's hand.

'This is my arrangement, dear,' he said gently. 'Hold your horses.'

'Paul didn't get very far,' said George, shaking his head, 'but it was our fault that it should happen at all. I'm sorry.'

Mr Brown pushed himself out of his seat and looked out of the window. 'Lovely place, this,' he declared. 'Let me tell you something –'

George interrupted with another attempted apology, but Brown raised a hand, half in acknowledgement, half for silence, and went on.

'When I was a kid I ran away from home because my old man treated my mother like a piece of dirt – that's a strong expression, but I mean it. So I ran off, and the police caught me and took me back. Mrs Brown and I have made a happy home for our Paul. He's got every advantage in life. Hard work's made me a millionaire and my wife's as loving a mother as you could ever find. And I do like this place. So the boy ran away and now he's come back – you didn't try and hide it from me, and I appreciate that, Mr Drummond. What's happened hasn't made a bit of difference to me wanting that memorial for my mother. I've given it a lot of thought, and what I've come up with is a music school – the Gertrude Brown Music School – and you'll get your new drains and whatever else you need. I'm not sending my son to a school to have the place close down at the end of his first term. I still want to look at the books, mind, but I'm sure everything'll be hunky-dory. The Gert Brown Music School' – he turned the title over appreciatively on his tongue – 'I like it.'

'I wonder. . .' George began hesitantly.

'Not having a change of heart, I hope, Mr Drummond?'

'On the contrary, Mr Brown. I was about to suggest that we might even get your mother down to open it.'

Brown beamed, his face as round and serene as a Buddha's.

'What a marvellous idea! Free enterprise! The Arts! Sciences! Learning! I do like all that. No use to me – but I like it.'

He rubbed his hands energetically, evidently unable to experience such enthusiasm without giving it physical expression.

'I can look at your books later, but what I'd really like to do right now is get outside and have a good poke around to see where we can excavate. I like a bloody good excavation,' he explained and, finding himself close enough to George, slapped him firmly on the shoulder. 'This is a great school. I said to my wife and I said to my mother, I knew I was going to get a kick out of Drummonds. Makes me wish I was a lad again. I like this place!'

'Yes,' George agreed. 'So do I.'

3

By squinting at the cover of her Pat Boone EP, Wendy could transpose Charles' even features on to the singer's handsome face, even though Charles' eyes were piercingly blue where Boone's were brown and his chin a degree or two more angular. She smiled at the idea of Charles slicking back his fair, straight hair or wearing white socks for anything other than tennis and cricket or allowing himself to utter words as ungrammatical as, 'Ain't had no lovin' since you know when', even if he expected her to believe him.

A knock at the door interrupted her thoughts, but she had no time to put down the picture or check that her dressing gown was wrapped properly around her, before Charles flung the door open with such force that the draught rattled the window and the needle hopped a whole chorus on the record.

'What the hell is all this about us being engaged?' he stormed.

Wendy pushed the collar of her dressing gown up to her chin and pulled her feet up under her on the bed, as if they were cold.

'Shut the door, Charles, please. Do you want the whole school to hear you shouting?'

Charles slammed the door, jolting the record to a premature end. Wendy's eyes flared.

'And I don't know what you're talking about,' she said angrily.

'The whole world is blathering on about you and me – engaged! Getting married!' He thrust his hand into his hair and let it rest there like a comb, hair sprouting between his fingers. 'Who have you been saying it to?'

'I haven't told anyone.'

Charles took his hand from his head, but some strands of hair remained untidily awry. He scowled at Wendy.

'Well, I certainly haven't – so it's got to be you. If you think it's some sort of half-baked joke, that's your affair, but I resent it.' He leaned over her threateningly, as he repeated his question: 'Who have you been talking to?'

'Charles, you're being incredibly cruel.'

'Me?' Charles demanded, backing away as if threatened himself. 'I haven't done a thing. I just object to being quizzed by my father about what he called my "secret plans" – asking me why I was keeping him in the dark about it. There's only one place these pathetic little rumours could come from – and that's you. At least have the decency to own up. Tell me what the hell you've been saying?'

'Please calm down, Charles,' Wendy suggested coolly. 'I don't know what's happened. I honestly don't. Did your father tell you how he heard?'

'Foster Gill.'

'General Gill told him?'

'He kindly informed my father of our engagement,' said Charles in a sour tone. 'So who told him?'

'I suppose if Foster Gill told your father, then it must've started with my uncle. He knows we've been out a lot. What's the point of keeping it secret? He must have assumed we're engaged. I can't see how else it could have happened. I'm sorry, Charles,' she added, 'if it's my fault.'

'Just because your uncle's a governor doesn't give him the right to gossip,' Charles hissed, forcing each word between his teeth. 'There's enough of it flying around the place without him.'

'I don't think he is a gossip. He's a judge – he's supposed to know what's right and wrong.'

'That's your opinion. Quite frankly, in front of that particular judge it's probably as well to keep your mouth shut.'

'Charles, I've said I'm sorry, and I mean it. But I will not be made a scapegoat for what you imagine other people may have said or done.' She stared hard at him to reinforce what she had just said, then looked away, turning her shoulders with her head, so that her back was to him. 'Now I think you'd better go.'

Charles made a tentative move to touch her, hesitated and reached for the door handle instead. In the silence they were both aware for the first time of the needle clicking and scraping in the last endless groove of the record.

Susan Pusey was setting up her easel in the empty art room when Binny's head appeared round the door.

'Mmm-mind if I come in?'

'Not if you don't mind if I carry on with what I'm doing.'

'Need to share the load.'

'Tim, you seem to talk in telegrams,' Susan observed with a gentle laugh.

'Too much time on the bridge,' Binny explained, edging his way between the tables towards the space Susan had cleared. 'At sea, language is a means of communication, and nothing more. The rest obscures the message. Most of what people say is mere ornamentation – why bother with it?'

'Literature would be fun if everyone followed your philosophy.'

'Different kettle of fish. Individual expression. Interpretation. Same with painting.' His gruff staccato speech softened. 'I'd like you to see my drawings some time, Susan. I think they're rather Russell Flint.'

'I can't until you show them to me.'

'Many takers for your art club?'

'More than I can manage – it's always the same. Why do you ask?'

Binny shrugged awkwardly.

'I haven't got a single name down for my Bible-reading club.'

'Then you've got Wednesday evenings free – lucky you!'

'But that's not what I want. Either it's a pretty grim reflection on the godless age we live in, that not one boy wants to read the Bible of his own accord, or it reflects on me.'

'Perhaps they just don't want to join a club to do it?'

'But what will the headmaster think?' He caught Susan's bemused look. 'I mean, of me – with absolutely no takers?'

'I'm quite sure he won't mind a bit. Tim, you mustn't take it all so personally.'

'I'm trying to do the best I can,' Binny went on gloomily. 'I make suggestions, but no one's interested. I don't think I'm much liked' – he paused before concluding – 'by the staff or the boys.'

'For God's sake, Tim, don't start wondering whether people like you or not.'

'You can understand how I feel, can't you?'

Susan's voice had risen impatiently with each reply; now she answered calmly, 'Of course I do.'

'You don't mind a chap pouring out something of what's on his heart?'

Susan tried to reassure him with a smile.

'If that's all you've got on your heart, then there isn't much to worry about.'

Binny shifted his weight uneasily from one foot to the other.

'Actually, there's rather a lot more.'

'Well, you can always have a talk to me about it, if you want. That seems to be one of my functions in life,' Susan muttered rather more wearily than she intended.

Throughout the preceding conversation, except when Binny's more exasperating remarks had distracted her, Susan had been preparing to paint, stocking a table by her easel with brushes, paints, turps, a palette knife and rags. Now she fetched a partly composed canvas from a cupboard adjoining the art room. She positioned it on the easel and stepped back to study it. Binny stood beside her and frowned at the unfinished, yet easily recognizable figures of Fordham, Heritage and Braithwaite.

'What a bunch,' he grunted. 'The Four Horsemen of the Apocalypse.'

'There are only three of them.'

'Not exactly beautiful.'

'Characters, though.'

'Superficial.'

Susan was careful to control her voice. 'Don't be so critical, Tim. Be positive. See what you like. Enjoy things.'

'I don't find much to enjoy. I don't think I was sent down to earth to enjoy myself, do you?'

'I really don't know. I wasn't responsible for sending you. For God's sake, don't worry about everything so much, Tim.'

'Someone has to,' Binny intoned ominously, and began to back away towards the door. 'And if it's me who has the duty to worry, I'll perform it. By Jove, I'll perform.'

He emphasized this last remark by raising his right forefinger high over his head, an absurdly theatrical gesture, especially for so small an audience, or one perhaps borrowed from the pulpit of a minister fond of melodrama. Whichever, it seemed entirely unnecessary to Susan, who was bothered enough by the substance of Binny's bizarre undertaking.

From behind, to Fordham, as he entered the art room followed by Braithwaite and Heritage, it looked as if Binny was pointing out some flaw in the ceiling plaster or blemish on the paintwork, and he said as much, with more than a hint of mockery in his voice. Binny began to mutter an explanation, but was hampered by an exceptionally high ratio of hums, and retreated from the room instead.

'I wish you wouldn't take the mickey out of him all the time, Chris,' Susan said reproachfully. 'It's cruel.'

'Nonsense, the man's a prig. He deserves everything he gets.'

'You must admit, Susan,' Braithwaite agreed, 'he is rather a queer fish. Today I came upon him sitting on a tree stump, prayer book in hand, conducting a one-man service.'

'He's a bit odd, yes, but you don't help. He's convinced no one likes him.'

'Maybe he's not such a fool after all.'

'Chris!' Susan warned severely.

'How's the masterpiece coming on?' Heritage

inquired, and peered at the canvas. 'I suppose you want us stock still and silent as usual?'

'No, you can talk today, as I'm not going to be working on the faces. That is, if you can find a subject you won't get too animated about.'

'Better leave Binny off the agenda then,' Fordham said with a grin. But added quickly, 'Sorry, Susan – subject closed.'

'Not much of the revolutionary in your pose, Bertie,' observed Heritage.

'The Major – a revolutionary?' Susan echoed in surprise.

'Him and his staff association. Haven't you heard?'

Susan looked inquiringly at Braithwaite, while he mounted the podium on which the trio posed for each sitting. The presence of a platform under his feet was appropriate, given the political nature of the short speech which followed.

'It's important, Susan,' Braithwaite began. 'I honestly believe that the staff here ought to form an association – a union of some kind. Frankly, the conditions of work are frightful and unless one has private means it's damned hard to scrape a penny by way of savings. But take Brown's cash, add organized pressure from us – and the result? Profitable use. Would the ladies' common room approve of a union?'

'No,' answered Susan flatly.

'They'd hate the idea,' Fordham agreed.

'Perhaps if we had a meeting?'

'Oughtn't you to talk to the headmaster first?' Heritage suggested.

'Oh no.' Braithwaite shook his head. 'Support from the other ranks first – then the headmaster. Besides, I've already outlined my ideas for modernizing the school.'

'How did George react?' asked Fordham.

'He told me we weren't running a country club,' Braithwaite answered drily, but provoked by the amusement on the faces of his audience adopted a more animated tone. 'Progress is not a concept George understands, which is why this school is stuck in the thirties. This is 1956 – and he's running the place on pre-war values.'

'I had no idea you were such a radical,' said Susan.

'It's not something he generally advertises,' Fordham explained. 'Hardly surprising, really. Can you imagine the reaction of ninety-nine per cent of Drummonds parents to a card-carrying Communist in charge of the coffers?'

'What makes you think the other one per cent would approve?' murmured Heritage.

'I am not a member of the Party,' Braithwaite stated carefully, 'more a fellow traveller. I happen to believe Stalin was pretty good organizationally.'

'Always believe a country should clean its stables once in a while?' Fordham pressed him.

Braithwaite ignored the question and rounded on Susan. 'What about you?'

'I'm not a politician. I prefer Gaitskell to Eden, but I prefer John Osborne to both. And I can't help thinking,' she added worriedly, 'that your staff association will cause trouble.'

'I was thinking of raising the matter at the next staff meeting.'

'Well, don't count on a quorum if the rest of the business takes too long,' growled Heritage. 'I certainly shan't give up any more of my lunch break than I absolutely have to. What's the meeting about anyway?'

'Fireworks.'

'Are you talking metaphorically, Bertie?' Fordham inquired.

Braithwaite raised his voice above the conversation in the common room. 'Matters arising – fireworks display and research. Siggy?'

Gunz stood up.

'If I may remind colleagues, it was decided to postpone apportionment of funds for research upon explosive substances until the appointment of a new colleague responsible for Scripture Union subscriptions. We now have to decide.'

'Whether we apportion monies to fireworks or the Scripture Union,' Braithwaite told the room. 'I think this is you, Commander.'

Binny was already on his feet, but drew himself an inch or two taller, a glance in Gunz's direction suggesting that his purpose was to draw attention to the doctor's lack of height.

'There can be no doubt that funds must not only be provided for the Scripture Union,' he said firmly and without preliminary impediment, 'but that they must be increased. We are talking of ten pounds – and I propose fifteen.'

'Unless I am supported, I cannot provide the traditional display on November fifth,' Gunz argued.

'It's a matter for the headmaster.'

'Actually, it isn't, Tim,' said Braithwaite. 'We have what we may call executive responsibility for this decision.'

'But I do need new Bible notes,' Binny appealed.

'Could I propose that discussion in Bible reading sessions in the club should be more free-wheeling?' Gunz glared at Binny. '*No* notes.'

'By all means propose it,' said Binny. 'I will counter-propose that experiment in Science be more, as you put it, more 'free-wheeling' and I daresay you, Dr Gunz, will protest. I believe you are opposed to atomic bombs. I doubt you will allow such free-wheeling experiment with atomic bombs in this school.'

'I am simply talking of explosive substances. By definition, atomic bombs are more dangerous than Bible reading notes.'

Binny pounced keenly on Gunz's statement. 'On the contrary, doctor. Out-of-date Bible-reading notes may infiltrate out-of-date notions of the faith on which this school is founded. Nothing could be more dangerous,' he declared.

While each man eyed the other defiantly, Susan said, 'Can I settle this by handing over the surplus from the art room to Siggy? That way he can get his dynamite and Tim can get his Bible notes.'

'It is not dynamite,' Gunz assured the meeting.

'While appreciating Miss Pusey's generosity,' said Binny, looking at Susan and reddening instantly, 'I don't wish to be the object of charity.'

'Merely hope and faith?' Heritage murmured from behind his paper.

'Look, this is the last item,' Braithwaite said impatiently, 'so can we bash on? Those in favour of Susan's proposal?'

Only Binny's hand did not rise.

'Well, Tim?' Braithwaite asked.

'A reluctant aye is all you'll get from me, Major.'

'Sounds unhealthy, doesn't it?' said Fordham. 'A reluctant eye. Definitely pinkish, I'd say, Bertie.'

'Not so much of the pink, Christopher,' warned Braithwaite, then resumed his chairman's voice. 'Motion carried. Any other business?'

'Only coffee,' said Susan quickly, at the sound of crockery clattering outside the door.

'Meeting closed,' Braithwaite announced unnecessarily, since Susan's words had effectively ended it already.

'Thank God for that,' muttered Heritage, motioning Gunz over to his armchair. 'Siggy, there's a filly running at Epsom this afternoon that I'd put a few bob on, if I were you.'

'Can you get to the bookie's before games?'

'If I'm quick.'

Gunz pulled a pound note from his wallet.

'Ten bob each way, I'd suggest, Siggy.'

'What's the horse's name?'

'Royal Floozie.' Heritage hauled himself cautiously from the depths of his ancient armchair. 'She's running in the three-fifteen.'

'Perhaps she'll turn out to be the answer to the fireworks research fund.'

'Fingers crossed,' said Heritage, crossing his own.

Catching the tail end of this exchange, Binny nudged Braithwaite covertly.

'I think it would be advisable to have a word with Heritage and Gunz about gambling.'

'Whatever for?' Braithwaite demanded.

'Not in the common room,' Binny went on. 'I am very much opposed to gambling. I've seen lives wrecked by it.'

'It's perfectly harmless, Tim,' said Braithwaite, more kindly. 'Surely you know a little of what you fancy does you no harm. All things in moderation.'

'I must declare my position,' Binny said insistently.

'If you want to speak to them about it, by all means do.'

'Then I will.' Binny's eyes lit with an evangelical fire and he formed a symbolic fist with his right hand. 'By Jove, I will.'

'But if you'll excuse me,' said Braithwaite, anxious to be out of the room, 'I have to see the headmaster.'

With two determined strides Binny confronted the gamblers.

'I think you two should know my views about betting,' he blurted. 'About gambling in general and most especially the passing of bets here in the common room.'

'And what are your views, Commander?' Gunz asked with exaggerated courtesy.

'It's intolerably bad form.'

'Really?' said Heritage wearily.

'And it must stop.' Binny beat the air in time with each syllable. 'Do you hear?' His voice rose above the sound of the bell.

Heritage joined the drift towards the door with an air of disinterest that infuriated Binny, but Gunz, after stooping to retrieve a pile of text books from the floor, faced him squarely.

'Yes, I hear you.' He spat the words with undisguised disdain. 'And I'm not going to listen to another word of your sanctimonious bosh. In future it will be best that you avoid talking to me entirely, because that is precisely what I shall be doing to you. I want nothing more to do with you.'

He remained where he stood for a few more moments in an attitude so tense with anger that it seemed only the books in his arms prevented his flying at Binny with both fists. Then he stumped from the room.

Binny blinked vacantly at the circle of empty chairs before he noticed Susan standing by the door. He opened his mouth, unsure of what to say, but aware of a nagging need to apologize. While he groped for words, she went; and Binny did not find another opportunity to explain himself until the end of the afternoon, when he found her in the art room. He sat on his hands on the edge of a sink and swung his feet beneath as he watched her paint.

'I can't sit on the fence, Susan. One has to stand up for one's beliefs – what else is there?'

'Try and accept people a bit more.' She looked at him across her palette, while she twirled a blob of paint with her brush. 'I think it might help you to study oriental philosophy.'

'I didn't serve against the Japs so I could end up sitting cross-legged on a cushion. Oh, no.'

'I was thinking of the Chinese – or you could study their art, like Van Gogh did.'

'He was a raving lunatic!' Binny exclaimed, appalled. He jumped from his perch and began to mooch among the scattered tables.

'Tim, please, can't you relax? Susan implored. 'I understand intensity and I understand passion, but this is only a boys' preparatory school. It isn't the centre of the universe.'

'Don't you understand dedication?'

'Of course. But you've only been here a few weeks. It's not a monastery. All we're doing is earning a living teaching the little buggers – don't let it go to your head.'

Binny stopped abruptly in his aimless circuit of the art room, and was almost hidden by the easel as he said in a hurt voice, 'You don't understand, do you?'

Susan's patience, already stretched by a busy timetable, twanged at Binny's tone, as much as his remark, and snapped.

'I'm trying to, Tim,' she said angrily. 'I'm also trying to paint, because I enjoy it. If you go on whining to everyone, you'll drive yourself dotty – like poor old Van Gogh. So just shut up, will you!'

She cursed under her breath and flicked at a clumsy brush stroke with the corner of a rag, remaining bent in front of the canvas until the sound of Binny's shoes disappeared, then because she was shaking, she put down her palette and sat down.

Susan's lack of sympathy, or so he saw it, was not, in fact, the cause of Binny's visit to the headmaster, as he had already arranged the interview of which the outcome was that Braithwaite, Gunz and Fordham had been rounded up by Charles, and now sat in George's study.

'Binny's convinced he's being persecuted,' George said. 'That may be somewhat extreme – I don't believe any deliberate Binny-baiting goes on, but I certainly don't like the way he's being treated, and I want to make it absolutely clear to all of you that I want the air of hostility surrounding him cleared up.'

'He is not a very co-operative man,' said Gunz.

'All of us, Siggy, are to a greater or lesser extent co-operative.'

'He's particularly prickly, George,' Braithwaite confirmed, 'and unqualified. In my opinion, if this school is to progress at all, it can do without men like Binny.'

'Indeed?'

'Yes, we need young people here,' Braithwaite went on with growing enthusiasm, 'like Charles – practical men. Doers. The entire country must rethink itself and so must we. Binny is simply not a man for the future.' He turned to Charles for confirmation. 'Is he?'

Charles was saved from taking sides by Gunz, who observed, 'I do see seeds of violence in his personality.'

'In that case you will be particularly careful not to

offend him,' George said deliberately. 'Is that quite clear? Well, is it?' he repeated, exacting a nod from each, before dismissing them with a firm 'Thank you'.

Charles got up to leave with the others, but his father called him back and told him, when the door had closed, 'I've got Binny an appointment with Leo this afternoon after school. He may simply be unwell physically, but I doubt it. At any event, we'll have the opinion of a professional. Then we shall see. Oh, and Charles' – he left his words dangling until he was sure of his son's total attention – 'don't encourage Bertie's more radical, sillier views.'

'We have to move with the times, father,' Charles protested, 'to be more contemporary, if we're to survive.'

'The word "contemporary" conjures up a kind of furniture of a particularly vile Festival of Britain hangover sort. Newness for no other reason than newness itself. Bertie's a romantic old socialist – a perfectly adequate bursar, but given to fits of change for change's sake.'

'Not unmodern,' persisted Charles. 'He does look into the future.'

'Leave that to the clairvoyants,' sniffed George.

'I'm serious.'

'So am I.'

'Very serious, father,' Charles repeated forcefully.

'Then I hope this seriousness includes Wendy,' said George. 'If so, well and good. If not, sort it out. I don't want to be surrounded by a regiment of weeping women.'

'There's only one.'

'One's quite enough, Charles,' George groaned. 'Do grow up, there's a good chap. Give maturing a try.'

*

'Come on, Pam,' said Pauline, flapping her unbuttoned coat impatiently. 'We'll miss that bus.'

'You go on, then. I'll catch up. I'm not leaving here without my lipstick on – it might be that conductor who looks like David Whitfield.'

'Square!' scoffed Pauline with a giggle.

'At least he can sing,' Pam shouted after her.

When it was dry, Pauline preferred to walk on the grass rather than the gravel so as not to scuff her shoes, and because the sun was warm she skipped every few steps, unless it was the memory of the way she had felt while Charles had stood beside her in the scullery and watched her wash up, not saying anything, just smiling, that made her feel so light on her feet. In spite of the weather she kept her coat on, because it was new and because it set off her eyes.

Her first impression of the hunched figure on the bench by the bus stop was that it must be a tramp, so she kept to the opposite side of the road as she approached, and several times looked back over her shoulder for Pam. She realized it was Binny in the same instant she noticed he was crying, although knowing his identity made her scarcely less anxious.

'Hello, sir,' she said softly as she crossed the road, fearful of alarming him, but since he made no response, she sat down beside him on the bench and put an arm across his shoulders, feeling them rise and fall as he wept. 'Don't cry, dear, it's not the end of the world.'

Binny looked up, rubbed his eyes violently with the heels of his hands, and stared blindly at Pauline.

'It's me, sir. Pauline – from the school.'

Binny made neither noise nor movement, but tears sprang in the corner of his eyes, where they swelled until the lids and lashes could hold them back no longer; as they splashed down across his cheeks, two more appeared in their place, except they could not be distinguished as individual tears, but rather as a steady stream, as if each eye had sprung a leak. Pauline was unnerved. She offered him a handkerchief, but he seemed not to see it, so she poked it between his unresponsive fingers, and when at last she saw Pam, she ran to her.

'Am I glad to see you.'

Pam looked beyond her to the bus stop.

'What's the matter?'

'It's that new bloke – he's crying his heart out. I've never seen anything like it. I tell you, there's something wrong with him.'

Back on the bench, with Binny between her and Pam, Pauline watched nervously as he twined her handkerchief tightly round his restless fingers. The only sign that he was aware of no longer being alone was a question, dragged out by an empty voice.

'Where am I?'

'At the bus stop,' said Pauline, as if explaining to a child. 'Where are you on your way to?'

'I don't know,' Binny answered hopelessly.

'That won't get you very far then.' Pauline's head turned in the direction of a distant rumble. 'You'd better make up your mind – the bus is coming.'

'What bus?' Binny asked, his eyes clouding with the effort of memory.

'We can't leave him here like this,' said Pam, taking charge. 'You run back to the school and find matron. I'll stay here and look after, er – d'you know, I can't remember your name.' She shook Binny slightly, without effect. 'Off you run,' she urged Pauline with a shooing motion.

She waved the bus on when it stopped, drawing stares from several passengers and turning the conductor's grin to a baffled frown, as he stood on the steps and jabbed the bell twice. The bus pulled away with a thick belch from its exhaust, which left the sickly smell of derv in the air.

'You'll be all right,' Pam comforted Binny. 'I get depressed too. I do. Something terrible. I reckon it's a lot to do with the cleaning polish – doesn't half make you dizzy.'

Pauline's progress was hampered by her shoes, which were not designed for running, and she was relieved to see the headmaster's car emerge into the road. She stood in its way and waved her arms, noting with a tingle of delight which made her smile despite the circumstances that the driver was Charles. The car pulled up in front of her.

'What's the matter?' Charles asked, his head cocked above his elbow in the open driver's window.

Pauline put on a serious face.

'It's that new master – he's at the bus stop, all upset.'

'Commander Binny?'

'That's the one. I was going to get matron.'

'Let me take a look at him first.' Charles ducked his head back in the window, leaned across and unlatched the passenger door. 'Come on, get in.'

'Mmmm,' Pauline murmured approvingly, as she slid across the seat. 'Lovely car.'

'It goes,' said Charles, and let the handbrake off with a jerk.

Binny had collected enough of his shattered thoughts to recall that he should have been on his way to the doctor's on the bus, and was persuaded without difficulty to stumble from the bench and collapse into the front of the car, while Pauline and Pam climbed into the back. Several times during the short ride to the village Charles' eyes trapped Pauline's in the rectangle of the rear-view mirror.

By the time they arrived at the surgery Binny was insisting feebly that he was well enough to enter alone, but Charles, more firmly set on accompanying the patient, took him by the arm and pushed him along the path.

The sight of Mary Prior behind the reception desk caused Charles to gawp, much as a naturalist might on spotting a species familiar from a certain habitat in quite another.

'Hullo,' she said, noting his reaction with a smile. 'Don't look so surprised. I'm Dr Hull's receptionist – as of next week, really. I'm just learning the ropes at the moment.'

'What wonderful news,' said Charles with evident pleasure.

Dr Hull opened his surgery door on this interchange of smiles.

'Know each other do you?' he asked, at once providing his own answer. 'Of course you do. Your lad's at Drummonds, isn't he, Mary? And this,' he said, turning to the strikingly unhappy figure excluded from the scene so far, like an actor without lines, 'must be Commander Binny. Come on through.'

'This is fortunate,' said Charles, the moment the surgery door was shut.

'What is?'

'Leo being the school doctor. It means we're bound to see a lot of you.' Charles could feel his cheeks colour. 'Must dash. Bye.'

'Goodbye.'

A snatch of a song found its way to Charles' lips in a whistle, which rose to a hunter's view halloo when Pauline waved from the car.

'I hope you don't mind me getting in the front,' she said, 'but I felt silly sitting in the back all on my own. Pam said she'd walk as she lives so close and didn't know how long you'd be in the doctor's.'

'Where to?' he asked, distracted by the hand she dangled between the seats.

'Oh, not far.' The hand brushed Charles' jacket on the way to her lap, and she leaned slightly towards him. 'I hope you don't mind.'

'Not at all.'

As Pauline touched his arm and told him where to pull up, Charles calculated that she could have walked the distance in less time than she had waited in the car.

'I only share the house,' she was explaining, 'with some girls from the radio factory, but I've got my own room.'

'I'll see you in,' said Charles, covering the dryness in his voice with a cough.

He followed her into the house and upstairs, aware of a scent he associated with girls in coffee bars and cinemas, and winced at the interior of her room, with its net curtains and nylon bedspread and cheap modern furniture of the kind his father had taught him to abhor, but he pretended to take an interest in the photos from magazines pinned untidily to the walls, all so crudely tinted that the boys with their Brylcreemed hair appeared to be wearing lipstick, while Pauline took off her coat and shoes and poked a match through the grill of the gas fire.

'There,' she said, as the panels began to glow. 'I do like it warm and cosy in here.'

'I mustn't stay,' said Charles, relieved to look at her face instead of the pouting delinquents on the wall.

'You could stay long enough for a drink, couldn't you? I've got some gin.'

Whether it was the brand – Charles did not recognize the label – or the fact that the glass had come from her dressing table, he smelled perfume as he took small sips of the spirit, which was mixed with less water than he liked.

'Nervous?' Pauline asked.

'No – why?'

'Because I am a bit.' She shaped a shy, punctuating smile. 'I mean, you here – with me – the headmaster's son. What would people think?'

'There's no reason for them to know.'

'What?'

'No reason for them to know I've been to see you. Anyway' – he took a sharp gulp from his glass and felt the gin burn his throat – 'I don't see why I shouldn't be here.'

'Wendy wouldn't like it,' Pauline suggested timidly.

'Wendy . . .' Charles began defensively, but was excused the need to offer an explanation.

'She's so pretty – I wish I was like her.'

'But you're pretty too.'

'D'you think so?'

'Yes, I do.'

'You've noticed me then, 'cause I've noticed you.'

'Yes, I've noticed you a lot.'

Each word seemed to eat away at the space between them. Without taking her eyes from Charles', Pauline sank slowly on to the bed and stroked the creases out of the cover beside her.

'D'you want to see my photographs?'

'If you like,' Charles mumbled and sat on the space she had smoothed, while she pulled a shoe box from under the bed and flipped off the lid. She took a handful of photographs and squared up their edges like a pack of cards, but Charles was looking at the soft, white skin on her neck as she separated one from the rest.

'That's my mum and my dad and my two brothers. At home – in Surbiton. Ever been there?'

'No, I haven't,' Charles replied automatically, unwilling to consider the question any more than inspect the photograph.

'It's not much of a place. It's dead, really.'

She had been holding the photograph for him to take, and looked round at him when he made no move to accept it.

'D'you fancy me?' she asked quietly, and kept her mouth a little open as she waited for the answer.

'Yes, I do,' Charles replied, hardly louder than a whisper.

'Because I fancy you like mad.'

As their mouths mashed together, they fell back across the bed, and Charles inched his hand upwards from Pauline's waist until he could feel a mound under the fabric of her blouse. She pulled away almost at once, leaving Charles embarrassed and on the point of apology, but she freed her hand from under him and quickly unbuttoned the blouse; then her hands disappeared behind her back and he saw the lacy cups of her brassiere come away from her skin, aware an inseparable second after that his own hand was being guided towards her naked breast. He gasped at her candour, and Pauline giggled.

'Don't pretend you haven't done this before, Charles.'

'Suppose I sack him?' said George, aiming the hypothesis more directly at himself than at the doctor who sat opposite him. 'The chairman of the board of governors won't like it one bit. But, on the other hand, can I trust him in front of the boys? What exactly is wrong with the man, Leo?'

Dr Hull spread his hands to indicate the difficulty of diagnosis.

'He claims he's subject to fits, though I feel he's exaggerating. He also says he never sleeps, and it does seem probable that he's been sleeping badly, given his overwrought condition, so I've prescribed a mild sedative both to help him sleep and as a stand-by in case he should feel particularly distressed during the day. Other than that, I don't know, George. I'm not a psychiatrist, and while I'm on the subject I don't think there's any hope of getting Binny to go and see one voluntarily, but I would guess the basic problem is an inferiority complex, which should be quite containable, provided the people around him help and make allowances.'

'How can I have a man who bursts into tears in front of the maids and all and sundry, and expect to get away with it?'

'The sedative will certainly help – as long as he takes it – and then with patience. . .'

'Patience?' George repeated irritably. 'All that manic Bible-bashing! If that's what we'd wanted, we could've appointed some sort of priest, but Binny's an amateur, a part-time apostle, and he's gothically miserable. What's the future for him?'

'That I can't tell you, George, I'm afraid, but I do know he's desperately keen to serve the school. If you and your staff were prepared to jolly him along, I'm sure it would work wonders.'

'Frankly, Leo, I'm not at all sure I'm prepared to take the risk. We've got enough jovial loonies about the place without having to accommodate the real thing. I won't be responsible for a genuine lunatic loose among the boys, so I can't see I've any choice but to tell him to pack his kit and depart.'

'The institution comes before the individual, eh?' Dr Hull observed with a sigh that gave away his own opinion.

'Drummonds does!' George barked back.

4

George suddenly smiled as he stirred his coffee, evoking a look of amused inquiry from Mary.

'It may surprise you to learn that I've broken a rule tonight.'

'A school rule?'

George tapped his spoon contentedly against the rim of the cup.

'One of my own.'

'Oh?' said Mary, prompting him with a show of surprise.

'I think it's bad form to offer invitations to dinner – '

'To widows?' she said instantly, squeezing her guess into the gap between George's measured words.

'Not widows per se,' he explained. 'Parents of boys in general – one doesn't want to be seen to have favourites. However, I thought your new job was sufficient excuse for a small celebration.' He surveyed the restaurant with a satisfied air.

'I don't have the same rules as you, and I do allow myself favourites,' she said emphatically, 'though oddly enough I don't have any – perhaps because I don't have any rules.' She paused, and looked pointedly at George. 'I ought to tell you something. I confess I didn't want to send Edward away from home.'

'For his sake or yours?'

'For his,' she answered quickly, then with reluctance, 'no, perhaps for mine too.'

'It's perfectly natural to feel like that,' George observed with easy concern, 'but there are great advantages. Sooner or later Edward will have to stand on his own feet, and I believe that a child at Drummonds gets a different perspective on the value of home in relation to the rest of the world. At least, I hope so,' he conceded.

Mary held his eyes steadily across the table.

'Aren't you just perpetuating a very old system of privilege and division?'

'You could say so,' George allowed her, although a flicker of a frown betrayed his irritation. 'On the other hand, people are free to do whatsoever they wish with their families, their children – within the law, at any rate.'

'So long as they are rich enough.'

'I know,' George agreed. 'And I think a time will come when the system will probably pack up. Perhaps it should. Perhaps we should abandon elites, hereditary privilege, the Monarchy, the House of Lords.'

'Why not?' Mary shrugged.

'Because for the time being the majority of people don't seem to want to get rid of those aspects of the system.'

'But it worries me that Edward will grow up with a blinkered vision in your monastic society – your world without women.'

'There are several on the staff,' George protested.

'I suppose I mean girls,' said Mary. 'It's the idea of Edward growing up in a world without girls that bothers me more. I think I find it vaguely unwholesome.'

'That's a bit strong, Mary.'

'Private boarding schools do seem to make it harder

for young men to adjust naturally to girls. Girls become something apart.'

'I think I managed all right,' George huffed.

'And your son? Charles?'

'I've never been aware of any awkwardness where women are concerned.'

This remark produced a faint smile, which George returned uncertainly, before signalling the end of the discussion, and of a passable, but overpriced dinner, with a glance at his watch.

As he helped Mary into her coat, he said, 'Ever thought of marrying again?'

'Not just for Edward's sake,' she replied, with a readiness that showed she had considered the question before.

'What about your own sake?'

'Ah, it takes two,' she said lightly. 'I'm certainly not searching for a husband, but if someone was to search, as it were, for me' – she paused, as if she might be savouring that possibility – 'that could be different.'

He followed her into the street, acknowledging with a stiff nod an overly obsequious bow from the waiter who held open the door, and was stopped abruptly in his tracks by the sight, on the opposite pavement, of Charles and the school maid Pauline glued in a public embrace which, for no reason that George could readily explain, other than an almost undetectable whiff of the sea some streets away, reminded him of a sailor on shore leave with a tart. The shock was supplanted by a sudden fear that Mary might also witness the shaming scene, but as she turned, only aware after several steps that he was not with her, he caught up, and even succeeded in covering his anger and confusion in the time it took him to take her home, although his distracted state made conversation awkward.

His mood was not improved by Charles' delay in returning to the school, his son's lateness confirming what the incautious show of familiarity in the street had suggested, and so he responded to a knock at his study door with involuntary abruptness and greeted Susan's entry with a glower.

'I saw the light on,' she explained hesitantly, but George did not answer, and she went on hurriedly. 'We must keep Tim Binny.'

'Must, Susan?' George asked coolly. 'He's not an easy man.'

'I don't think any of us are, do you?'

'Some are easier than others.'

Susan eyed the seat usually offered in interviews with the headmaster, but receiving not even a flicker of encouragement, remained standing.

'But the staff will help him,' she pleaded. 'It's as important to care for the staff as it is to care for the boys, and I'm certain if he were to go – to be forced out – then there would be renewed calls for a staff union.'

'Are people talking about it?' George demanded, with the first evidence of interest in the conversation.

'It gets talked about.'

'By whom?'

'Bertie,' she answered easily. 'Some sort of union or association to protect employees' interests.'

'Are you serious?'

'Perfectly. I know you'd prefer me to tell you what's in the air, and I'm positive Tim's sacking would precipitate the whole thing.'

'Tim hasn't been sacked,' George said wearily.

'It's in the air.'

'Yet,' he added, emphasizing this qualifying coda with a frown.

Susan twitched uncomfortably under George's glare

and tugged at the ends of dark hair which framed her face.

'I only wanted to tell you what's in the air.'

'Susan, would you mind not using that phrase again. Your job is art. Art is not a political activity. Perhaps it is in the back pages of the *New Statesman*, but it's not here. It's a hobby, which is why we keep it safely in the art room.'

This attack seemed to re-establish Susan's resolve, because she said firmly, 'I only feel we should be fair to Tim.'

'We will be fair to Tim,' said George, gathering himself in his chair in a way that conveyed clearly to Susan that their meeting was about to end, 'if he's fair to us first, and begins to fit in. Thank you, Miss Pusey.'

George left his study soon after Susan to continue his increasingly rancorous vigil in his sitting room and when, after countless glances at both the watch on his wrist and the clock on the wall, noises in the hallway outside alerted him of his son's return, he rose, crossed the room and threw open the door before Charles had the buttons of his overcoat undone.

'What in God's name do you think you're doing?' he bellowed, all his pent-up anger exploding in the question.

'Going to bed,' Charles answered with a mixture of innocence and surprise.

'Don't you dare cheek me,' his father thundered. 'Get in here.' George held the door open for Charles to enter, and closed it behind him. 'Sit down.'

'Why?' Charles protested. 'Look –'

'Don't tell me to look, Charles,' George interrupted bitterly. 'I've already looked and seen all I need. I saw you with that maid – pawing her. . . kissing. . .'

'Father, do calm down,' Charles suggested with an air of reason which incensed George. 'You'll wake the boys.'

'I don't care if I wake the whole country,' George shouted, adding with an effort at self-restraint, 'but I do care that you seem to find it necessary to molest a school servant.' He caught his son's bewildered look. 'Don't hedge about. I saw you, Charles. I was in town with a parent. You were canoodling in full view of anyone who cared to look with that girl who washes up. What's her name?'

'I don't know what you're talking about,' Charles persisted stubbornly. 'You haven't had one too many, by any chance?'

'I know I've seen one thing too many,' George said, shaking his head as if his anger had given way to deep disappointment. 'By God, what would your mother have thought? What would anyone think? You stand to inherit this school, the goodwill of hundreds of families, their children, a future, a secure life. But if you think that entitles you to behave in a way that is not only immoral and offensive to the Christian spirit, but is disgraceful in every respect, then, so help you, you are mistaken.'

'What I do with my private life is my own affair,' Charles replied with quiet defiance.

'Is it, by God?' George's face darkened again. 'What if you get the girl pregnant? What if the whole disgraceful matter is gossiped about from here to everywhere? Do you realize what you're doing, Charles? You're breaking up the very fabric of the place. But you won't get away with it.'

'Get away with what, father?' Charles asked, persevering with his innocent tone.

'You know damn well what I'm talking about.'

'Father, dear father, I haven't got a clue,' Charles said, and went on soothingly, 'Tell me what's the matter, please. Let me try and help you. I hate to see you in such a dreadful state of nerves. I do hope you're not catching what Binny's got.'

'That's enough,' George snapped.

'No, it isn't enough. What am I meant to have done? Tell me. What exactly is the matter?'

George lowered his head.

'Have you – ' he began slowly.

'Have I what?'

'Slept with her?'

He looked up at Charles, who held his testing gaze easily.

'With whom?'

'The maid – and Wendy too, I suppose?'

'Look, father,' said Charles, 'I'm giving my life to our school. I live here and I sleep here alone. As I expect you sleep alone – unless, of course, you see fit to crawl out at night and offend against your own rules by sleeping with that very attractive blonde mother, what's her name? Mary Prior? Very pretty, isn't she?' He smiled as his father's brow furrowed. 'Don't think I haven't noticed.' He paused, prolonging the teasing smile, and introduced a tone of elaborate concern into his voice. 'You must be tired – it's late for you. Why don't you pop off to bed? Try and get a good night's sleep. I think I'll do the same. Things'll seem different in the morning, you'll see. Good night.'

George did not reply, but clenched and unclenched his fists several times before letting his hands drop loosely over the arms of the chair. Then he leaned his head against its back and closed his eyes, as if submitting to a sudden and intense exhaustion. Anyone entering the room would have thought him asleep, but his somnolent expression hid a mind that seethed with angry doubts and worries, about Charles, about Mary, about what Susan had said and about Binny, about his school, about himself.

5

'What were you in, Sykes?' George asked the young man standing tensely at ease in his study.

'REME, sir.'

'In that case you should've learned more than enough to cope with most things you'll come across as school handyman. But don't you think you'll find it rather different from National Service?'

Sykes grinned. 'That's what Pauline says.'

'Pauline?' George asked sharply, adding an interrogatory glance at Braithwaite.

'I forgot to tell you, headmaster,' said Braithwaite, smiling. 'Young Andrew here is an old friend of one of our maids. You know Pauline – pleasant girl.'

'Of course,' said George, and turned again to Sykes. 'You know her well, do you?'

'We're just good friends, as they say, sir,' the young man replied with another, broader grin. 'We've been courting quite a while.'

'You have a driving licence?'

'Yes, sir.'

George looked at Braithwaite, who responded with a satisfied nod.

'Well, I must admit that the job will be a fairly menial one,' George said, 'but if you're prepared to make a go of it, I'm sure you'll find it quite rewarding –

and you'll certainly be helping us out. I assume you're free to start at any time.'

Sykes nodded. 'Yes, sir.'

'In that case, the job's yours.'

'Thank you very much, sir,' Sykes said happily.

'Miss Fisher will tell you everything you need to know,' George added, with a vague wave towards the door. 'And I'm sure you'll be able to get Pauline to show you round.'

'Thank you, sir.'

When Sykes had gone, Braithwaite slid a sheaf of papers across George's desk.

'I've got something for him to do right away, George.'

'And what's that, Bertie?' George inquired, as he turned the pages in front of him.

'The guttering,' Braithwaite explained. 'That quote for replacing it is astronomical.'

'Something will have to be done,' said George, letting the pages fall back through his fingers. 'If there's one occupation I want to cease in this school, it's the business of dotting buckets about the place to catch the rain.'

'Guttering is a simple matter of the application of physics,' Braithwaite countered confidently. 'Liquids flow downwards – that's all.'

'Brown's man seems to think there's rather more to it than that.'

'One end up, the other end down,' Braithwaite continued. 'We could save damn near a hundred quid if we got young Sykes to do it. I'll supervise the work. I do know about guttering, George.'

'Instead of getting Brown's firm to do it?'

'Precisely.'

George fixed Braithwaite with a tired smile.

'Not so very long ago, Bertie, I recall you advocating everything from a cinema to a swimming pool with the aid of Brown's generous injection of capital. Clearly his cash hasn't stretched quite as far as you were counting on.'

'It's because we're not operating at a profit. In spite of Brown's money we're merely ticking over. And come the next capital crisis in, what, three years? Four perhaps, if we're lucky? What then? We'll be back where we started. We must start to operate at a profit.'

'That's rather a capitalist observation,' George remarked.

Braithwaite ignored the jibe, and went on, 'We need more children. We can't get away with another fee increase, so we must pack in more children.'

'Children?' George repeated hesitantly, as if he had encountered a new word.

'Girls, George,' Braithwaite said with great enthusiasm. 'Have you ever thought about girls? One half of the human race,' he added helpfully.

'No.' George pronounced the word determinedly.

'Why not?' Braithwaite persisted.

'When the day comes that I am replaced by a headmistress, I can quite see that girls may find their way in here,' George explained without conviction. 'One has to begin at the top. And as long as I am headmaster we remain all male.'

'Financial necessity, headmaster,' Braithwaite argued in a tone clearly intended to convey the desperate urgency of the situation. 'Stay put and we sink, change and we swim. Necessity compels us.' He banged the arm of his chair to drive home this point, splintering the wood with a gasp of surprise and pain.

'Another job for young Sykes,' George commented, while Braithwaite took turns at rubbing his injured hand and fiddling ineffectually with the broken halves of the chair arm.

'We remain in a state of serious financial crisis,' Braithwaite muttered.

'I know, Bertie,' George agreed, as grim-faced as his bursar. 'Things are falling apart. An increase in numbers is a solution, but let's not resort to extreme remedies such as girls. It really isn't an answer.'

Andy was propped against the pillows on Pauline's bed, his knees drawn up to support a newspaper whose pages he flipped over with one hand while the other ferried a cigarette between the corner of his mouth and an ashtray at arms' length on the bedside table. When Pauline walked in, he pointed at a photo in the paper of a dressing-gowned male and a female in a baby doll outfit, their limbs angled in a wild dance, and sneered.

'You'd think those toffs would've been brought up to know better,' he observed with distaste, while Pauline peered through a screen of cigarette smoke. 'Pyjama parties! What will they think of next?'

'She might have her undies on underneath,' Pauline suggested.

'Not her type,' Andy asserted with a shake of his head, then folded the paper and tossed it to the foot of the bed. 'Where've you been anyway?'

'Doctor's,' said Pauline, turning her back and occupying herself with the removal of her coat and shoes.

'Something up, is there?'

'No.'

'Could've fooled me,' Andy grumbled.

Pauline turned to face him.

'He told me I was very fit,' she said, pulling a taut

smile. 'Shouldn't have any trouble. Congratulations, he says, your husband will be pleased. Sarcastic old sod – he knows I'm not married. I could've kicked him.'

Andy squinted at the stub of cigarette he held delicately between the tips of his thumb and forefinger, puffed once more from it sharply, and squashed the end in the ashtray.

'Well?' Pauline asked, and when he said nothing, went on. 'I know whose it is. It's not yours – I worked it out. I've missed twice. First time I didn't think anything, I've never been all that clockwork. Then I missed again. That means it couldn't've been you – you weren't back. There's only one bloke it could've been.'

Andy swung his legs across the bed.

'Don't hit me, Andy,' Pauline begged.

'I don't hit women,' he replied flatly.

'Well,' said Pauline after a painful pause, clapping her hands with a show of brightness which her trembling mouth belied. 'That's two things to celebrate then, isn't it? Your job and my baby. Where shall we go, eh?' Her voice wavered crazily as it rose. 'Fancy going jiving? I feel like a really good time, don't you? A really terrific night out!'

Unable to control either her voice or her tears a moment longer, she collapsed, crying noisily, in the chair by the gas fire. Andy watched silently, then dropped to his knees at her feet, and pulled her head gently against his chest. Nothing more was said until she had finished crying and prised herself carefully away from him. Then she took a hand mirror from the narrow shelf over the fire, examined her reflection critically, and said, 'I'm a mess, Andy. I should look like this all the time.' She looked from the mirror to his face. 'I'm sorry, I really am. But you weren't here, were you? You were off in Germany. And I can't help being attractive, can I? You wouldn't want me if I wasn't, would you. I know I shouldn't have, I know it was wrong, and I know I'm landed with it. It was all my fault, I know, but I need you, Andy, I do.'

Andy held her knees and rocked them tenderly from side to side.

'It wasn't your fault, girl. I don't blame you. It was his fault. It's the feller's responsibility.'

'I didn't just mean that,' Pauline said, putting down the mirror and laying her hands on his.

'Don't worry so. We'll get over it.'

'I won't get rid of it, Andy,' she whispered earnestly. 'You know I couldn't do that.'

'I should hope not,' Andy said, pulling away slightly. 'I don't approve of that sort of thing. I don't approve of you either, girl, but it's not right you should be landed this way. The feller pays, that's my rule.'

Pauline took his hands from her knees and held them against her face.

'I love you, Andy,' she murmured, her eyes shining.

'So you say, girl,' he replied softly. 'And I love you.'

'Have you come about the broken chair, Sykes?' Dorothy asked, looking up briefly, but without interrupting the rapid staccato of her typewriter.

'I want to see Mr Drummond.'

Dorothy frowned at him over the top of her glasses.

'There's absolutely no need. I can show you the damage. It's quite obvious anyway, since the arm has practically detached itself from the rest of the chair.'

'I want to see Mr Drummond,' Andy repeated firmly. 'It's personal.'

'Well, I'm afraid he's working,' Dorothy answered in a voice that discouraged contradiction.

'He can't be teaching,' Andy insisted none the less. 'I checked the timetable.'

'That doesn't mean he isn't busy, Sykes,' Dorothy said irritably, but Andy made no move to leave. 'Very well, I'll see. Wait here.' She picked up her pen from the desk, as if to imply that Andy could not be trusted to leave it where it lay, and took it with her into the headmaster's study, returning a few moments later to mutter doubtfully, 'If it's really personal, you'd better go in.'

'Thank you for seeing me, sir,' Andy said as soon as he was in the room.

'I gather this is personal, Sykes.'

'Yes, sir.'

'Well, sit down,' George suggested pleasantly.

Andy positioned an upright chair opposite the headmaster's desk and sat erectly on it, gripping his hands between his thighs.

'I need your advice, sir,' he said. 'I'm not sure what I should do.'

'What's the matter?'

'It's my girl.' He hesitated. 'Pauline – the one who works here.'

George nodded. 'I know.'

'She's got herself in the family way – and not because of me.'

The angle of George's trunk tilted several degrees forward.

'You're quite sure of this?' he asked sternly.

'Oh yes, sir, the doctor's told her she's expecting, and I wasn't around at the time it must've happened. But the thing is, I want to marry the girl.'

'That's very decent of you,' said George carefully.

'I do love her, you see,' Andy explained, shifting slightly on his seat, 'even though she is a bit of a wild thing. I just love her – and she loves me. But the thing is, this baby. Now, I'll give it my name and I'll bring it up as my own, that's all right, but there's this other bloke, see –'

'And the responsibility is his.'

'That's right, sir,' Andy agreed. 'It is.'

'Do you know who he is?'

'Yes, sir.'

'Has Pauline spoken to him?'

'No, I have, just a few minutes ago – that's why I've come to see you.'

'What did he say?'

'He denied it, said he never did it, told me what I could do with myself, which put me in a spot. But I know who I believe, Mr Drummond, and it's not him. So what do I do?'

'Can you tell me who the man is?'

'I'm afraid you're in for a shock, sir,' Andy warned, 'because it's a member of your staff.' He seemed to wait for a word or a sign to continue, but George did not even blink. 'Mr Fordham.'

'Mr Fordham?' George repeated the name incredulously, then, with all the abruptness of a man who suddenly suspects a hoax, added, 'You do know who you mean?'

'Oh yes,' Andy replied in a voice unaffected by doubt.

'This is a very grave allegation, Sykes. I have to ask you whether you realize quite how serious it is?'

'I don't want to cause trouble, Mr Drummond,' Andy said in the same even tone. 'What's happened has happened.'

'Let bygones be bygones?'

'That's right, sir. And I'm going to stand by Pauline. But a baby isn't a bygone, is it? A baby costs money.'

'I think I'd better speak to Pauline before I do anything else,' said George.

Andy looked indignant.

'It's not that I disbelieve what you've just told me, Sykes,' George explained with a placatory smile, 'but I'd like to hear Pauline's own explanation. Would you fetch her for me, please?'

While he waited to interview the maid, George stood at the window and surveyed the school grounds, as he often did when every drawer of his desk seemed to store an unpleasant surprise. There was something reassuringly serene about the trees and lawns, a timelessness, as if Drummonds had always existed and always would. Financial crises could not tear the leaves from the trees or turn the grass less green. But the same view was not now a source of reassurance; the scene did not appear eternally impervious to the damage that could be caused by sexual indiscretion. George turned back, troubled, to his desk as Dorothy ushered in the maid with an air of disapproval.

'I want to get the details absolutely clear,' he said once he had heard Pauline's account. 'You were drinking in the Little Rose with your friend. And this was during the summer holidays?'

'August some time.'

'And Mr Fordham was in there,' George continued, 'and when your friend went, he came over to you?'

'Yes.'

'Why didn't you go with your friend?'

'She was meeting her feller – she didn't want me along.'

'So you were feeling left out of things, without a man, and there was Mr Fordham,' George pressed her.

'Yes.' Pauline checked herself. 'No, it wasn't like that.'

'You say Mr Fordham came over to you. Why do you think he did that?'

'I don't know,' Pauline shrugged. 'He just did.'

'You see, Pauline, I find it a little difficult to believe that Mr Fordham, a man I know extremely well, should approach you without some encouragement from you in the first place.'

'I don't know what you mean,' Pauline said uneasily.

George shook his head as he said, 'Bluntly, he isn't the type.'

Pauline resisted the suggestion silently for some seconds, then capitulated with a sigh.

'All right,' she said, although her eyes were defiant, 'so I smiled at him. I wanted to see if I could get him to buy me a drink – and I could. I chatted him up and we got along really well, and when he said could he walk me home, I couldn't see any reason why he shouldn't. So we got back to my place and he said, very politely, could he come in. I could've said no, but I thought, why not?'

'In other words, you seduced him.'

'Look, Mr Drummond, I'm not denying it, but none of that matters really. It's the baby that matters, and it takes two to make a baby.' Pauline paused to drive home her point. 'Whatever I did, Mr Fordham did too, and it's not fair of him to pretend it hasn't got anything to do with him. It isn't fair on me and it isn't fair on Andy.' Saying his name seemed to shake her self-control, and she started to sob as she went on, 'I know he's going to marry me, but that's because he's a good man, and it's just not fair on him.'

'All right, Pauline,' George said hurriedly, embarrassed by her tears. 'Not to worry, I'll speak to Mr Fordham.'

Before he did, he took the opportunity to confront

Charles with the news of Pauline's pregnancy, suppressing Fordham's identity long enough to prompt a startled denial of responsibility from his son, and allowing him to endure several more moments in a cold sweat of consternation in the hope that a lesson might be learned. Unfortunately, though not unexpectedly, Fordham was equally emphatic in his denial, and reacted to George's accusation and subsequent suggestion that he should resign quietly with a display of injured innocence which culminated in a threat of legal redress. When George withdrew to the window after Fordham's acrimonious departure from his study, it appeared that autumn's advance had accelerated unnaturally.

6

Sir Foster Gill banged his gavel and the murmur of conversation subsided.

'This is an extraordinary meeting of the board of governors. Any apologies?' he asked Braithwaite, who sat beside him.

'Councillor Simpson, Mr Ablett Rainer, Admiral Kelsey,' Braithwaite read from a list.

'So we have a quorum?'

'We do, sir.'

Gill turned from Braithwaite and addressed the sombre faces that ringed the table. 'The matter before us concerns a member of staff, Christopher Fordham.' His eyes settled on George. 'If you would like to give us your report, headmaster?'

'Thank you, chairman,' said George. 'Briefly, Fordham has made one of the school maids pregnant. The girl in question is engaged to be married to one of our maintenance staff. I received a complaint from the man. If you've read page three of my paper . . .' He left his statement unconcluded, while papers were rustled busily.

'Everyone read it?' Gill asked.

'One moment, chairman,' said Judge Deacon, raising a delaying finger. He scanned the page before announcing with a nod of approval, 'Good paper, headmaster.'

'Thank you, sir.'

'The headmaster quite properly has asked Fordham to resign,' Gill explained. 'Fordham has taken the advice of his solicitor.'

'Name?' Deacon inquired.

'Lasko.'

Deacon sucked in his breath sharply.

'I say, he's top-notch, Sir John Lasko.'

'Can we shift Fordham? That's the question,' said Gill. 'After all, suppose it gets about that one of our masters has got a maid in the family way.' He shook his head at the prospect. 'Not good at all. Comments around the table? Judge?'

'Standards must not be allowed to fall,' Deacon declared. 'An example of this kind is poor. On the other hand, if Lasko says his client denies the charge, I don't recommend tackling him in court.'

'Wing Commander?'

This invitation to speak brought Wing Commander Nee bolt upright in his seat, snapping to sedentary attention.

'It's a very difficult question, to which we must strive for the simple answer,' he suggested grandly.

'Which is?' asked Gill.

'School first, reputation second,' he said, as if the answer had been obvious. 'Third, the decent thing. All we fought for.'

'I'm not quite clear where you stand, Wing Commander,' Gill said.

'As a bachelor I have clear views, Sir Foster. The family needs to be cared for.'

'I think the wing commander has a good point,' Deacon agreed. 'On the one hand there is morality and on the other there is reputation – they sleep uneasily together.'

'The young lady is getting married, we are led to believe,' Lady Morell cut in briskly.

'Is she?' said Deacon thoughtfully. 'In that case, why can't she be paid off and Fordham kept on? She's getting married, so it's not as if she's being thrown out on to the streets.'

'Punish the girl and let the man get off scot-free?' George demanded with obvious disapproval. 'Just because he has Sir John Lasko on his side?'

'Discretion is essential,' Lady Morell advised. 'Have they accommodation to go to?'

'I believe not,' said George.

'Then let us accommodate them,' suggested Lady Morell. 'Let the school provide the family with a home, in return for which they will agree to drop their charges against Christopher.'

'Headmaster?' Gill prompted George.

'An excellent notion,' George admitted drily. 'Unfortunately there is no such accommodation, nor indeed has the school the funds to provide any.'

A tic of irritation tweaked one corner of Lady Morell's tightly pressed lips, as the chairman passed on to the other members of the board for their opinions.

In the unlikely event that George had been called upon to explain the cause of his bleak mood that evening to the board, he would undoubtedly have attributed his ill humour in its entirety to having been dragged up to London at short notice to attend that very meeting. Such apparent honesty would nevertheless have concealed another reason. On his night off, as it should have been, he had arranged to take Mary Prior to the cinema, a date he had only remembered to break by telephone that afternoon.

'Your poor father,' Dorothy had muttered sympathetically, when she described George's predicament to Charles, but Charles' thoughts had not been with his father.

After consulting the local paper for programmes and times, he had presented himself at Mary's door at an appropriate hour and answered her cautious welcome with his widest smile. He was wearing one just as broad while he watched her pour coffee in her drawing room several hours later.

'How about something continental next time?' he said, stretching comfortably against the sofa cushions. 'One of those new Italian films perhaps?'

'Or Brigitte Bardot?' asked Mary, as she handed him a cup.

'Why not?' said Charles happily. His arm lay along the back of the sofa; Mary chose another seat.

'No,' she said.

'No?' Behind his grin Charles' voice was surprised.

'No next time, Charles. When you came, you offered yourself as first reserve – your own words – and that's what you stay.'

'But I don't feel like a reserve any more,' Charles protested. 'I want to get to know you.'

'It wouldn't be a good idea,' Mary said firmly.

'Nonsense.' Another grin. 'D'you know, I think I prefer older women.'

'If that's a genuine observation, then let me tell you older women like to be preferred, but not because they are,' she said with a tone of gentle admonition, 'as you so engagingly and frankly put it, older. At least, this older woman doesn't want to be told it.'

'I'm sorry.' Charles looked contritely into his coffee cup.

'Don't be,' Mary advised him. 'Never apologize to a

woman if there's nothing to apologize for other than being honest.'

'I must admit . . .' Charles faltered.

'What must you admit, Charles?'

'I do fancy you.'

Mary smiled as she watched Charles gulp coffee.

'You're not the first,' she replied without a trace of conceit or coquettishness.

'I don't expect I'll be the last either.'

Mary corrected him less warmly than before. 'Wrong move again, Charles. You see, it's up to me, isn't it, to decide who'll be the last. I think you'd better finish your coffee.'

Charles took several sips, then stopped to ask, 'Are you seriously interested in my father? Or is there someone else?'

'I'll pretend you didn't ask that.'

'But I'd like to know.'

Mary stood up.

'Dear Charles,' she said, as if she was addressing a fond, but tiresome child. 'Good night.'

Charles' cup and saucer clattered on the table top and he got hurriedly to his feet. In spite of his dismissal, he grinned again.

'I'll see myself out.'

'Yes,' Mary answered, smiling. 'And thanks for the evening.'

'Not at all.'

His grin seemed to leave an afterglow hovering in the doorway.

The effect of Charles' mild telling-off was titillating, rather than hurtful, and did nothing to diminish his jubilant mood, which contrasted sharply with his father's scratchy state, when he found him at the house, staring at the fire through a glass of whisky. George raised the glass an inch by way of a greeting and launched at once into a tirade.

'What an utter waste of an evening. The board decided absolutely nothing. I sat listening to more pious rubbish than one could imagine it possible to invent, and every one of them terrified of this spiv of a lawyer. And as for that Lady Morell – I curse the day I ever accepted Gill's idea we have her as a governor. Damn woman!' he concluded vehemently.

While his father was speaking, Charles had slipped his scarf from his neck into his pocket, adjudging an inquiry into his own activities inadvisable in the light of his father's humour.

'What exactly did Lady Morell say?' he asked.

'Some cock-eyed idea that we give the couple room here and accommodate them,' he growled. 'Why, oh why should I be put in the position, with no funds in the bank, of having to provide a maintenance man who's hardly been here long enough to draw his first pay and his trollop of a wife and their blasted offspring with a roof over their heads, when it's my maths master who's got her in the family way? Where is the sense in it?'

'Hasn't Lady Morell something to do with Lady Arabella Waterstone? Isn't she her godmother or something?'

'What the hell's that got to do with anything, Charles?' George demanded angrily.

'It hasn't really,' said Charles. 'I only mention the connection because of Siggy.'

'Charles, you may not have noticed, but I am not in a good mood,' George explained slowly, fixing his son with an irascible eye. 'First you bring up Lady Waterstone, now you mention my science master. Any more red herrings you'd like to introduce into the conversation? Or perhaps you'd be kind enough to explain yourself?'

'Surely you've heard?'

'Heard what, Charles?'

'About their engagement.'

'I am not in the mood for jokes or riddles,' George warned, 'but if you're trying to tell me that that old fogey is going to marry one of the wealthiest, most elegant women in the county – '

'That's exactly it,' said Charles. 'Siggy and Lady Arabella are engaged. Quite extraordinary, isn't it?'

'It's utterly preposterous – not to mention the fact that masters are supposed to ask my permission to marry.' George looked hard at Charles again. 'Are you absolutely certain about this?'

'There was a staff celebration in the common room, father. Siggy bought a bottle of sherry – and he wouldn't have done that without good reason,' Charles added meaningfully. 'And I understand there was a somewhat more exclusive do at Lady Arabella's. Only Christopher got invited.'

'I don't want to hear that man's name again today,' George groaned.

'He's well in with her crowd, you know,' Charles continued, ignoring his father's request. 'It was he, evidently, who played Cupid to the happy couple. And if he knows Lady Arabella, he may well be acquainted with her godmother. Friends in high places, father, if one could call the board of governors of Drummonds a high place.'

'Come back for your key, Andy?' Pauline called in answer to the knock. She slid lazily off the bed, poked her toes into a pair of his slippers, and shuffled to the door. As soon as she opened it, she squealed in shock and tried to push it shut, but Fordham was already forcing his way in.

'Go away, Christopher,' she hissed.

'I saw Sykes go out,' said Fordham breathlessly, his face shining with perspiration. 'We've got to talk, Pauline.'

'I haven't got anything to say to you,' Pauline replied sullenly.

'You do know what it is you're doing to me?' he demanded. 'You do realize I'm broke, don't you? And there'll be no money in it for you?'

'It was stupid you coming here.'

'Not at all,' Fordham insisted. 'The headmaster's accused me of making you pregnant. Now I'm damn sure I can't have been the only lover you entertained. I know there were others – maybe not at exactly the same time, but as near enough as dammit to make it impossible for you to make a case against me. Or anyone else, for that matter. Do you understand what I'm saying?'

'I'm not listening,' said Pauline. 'And you'd better go.'

'I'm not going until I've finished, and I'd advise you to listen.' He tried to grab her wrists, but she snatched them away and turned her back on him, covering her ears with her hands, so he leaned towards the side of her head when he spoke again. 'What I'm saying is, there's going to be some very nasty legal proceedings.' He bent closer to her ear. 'In public. I'm going to name as many names as I can, and knowing what little I do about Andy, and I think it's enough, I don't think he's going to want to marry a girl with the reputation I'll give you, but then you didn't have to put my livelihood on the line.' He stepped back and let the menace drain from his voice. 'I'm sorry it had to come to this, I really am. And you always said you were a girl who could keep a secret.'

If George had given no more than momentary attention to his son's flippant count of the links in a social chain that connected Fordham to Lady Morell, he was obliged not only to reconsider Charles' conjecture, but to contemplate an ancillary connection besides, when Lady Arabella telephoned to request a meeting between George, herself, and Sir John Lasko. The existence of this last association was quickly confirmed by a familiarity from which George, in his own sitting room, was excluded.

'Drummond,' Lasko greeted George with the chilly formality of one who is about to sue the other. 'First of all let us agree that this meeting is without prejudice, off the record, and in the nature of an exploration.'

'Beautifully put, John,' Lady Arabella observed.

'Agreed,' said George stiffly.

'And now that the formalities are over,' said Lady Arabella, 'I would like to offer my modest proposition. True, Christopher slept with a servant.'

'Objection,' Lasko protested, but Lady Arabella overruled him with a perceptive smile, and continued.

'And the servant, equally clearly, slept with him. It was not in the nature of some rather louche rape. However, if Christopher is forced to admit the whole thing, it will put him in a very unpleasant position. And if the Press get hold of it –'

'Which they will,' interrupted Lasko, and directed an unambiguous warning glance at George. 'Have no doubt.'

'Poor Mr Drummond will face a horrid stink,' Lady Arabella concluded with exaggerated concern.

'There's a simple solution, Drummond,' said Lasko. 'Give the girl her notice, pay a sum in respect of inconvenience, Drummonds meets my costs, and we expunge the whole thing from Christopher's record.'

'I will not sack the girl.'

'Of course not,' Lady Arabella agreed. 'Suppose instead that the girl and her young man were to be given a little flat – *bijou* – the gardener's cottage, as it were.'

'This charming rustic notion no doubt comes from Lady Morell?' George inquired drily.

'I have spoken to her,' Lady Arabella replied.

'Then you will be in no doubt also that no such *bijou* accommodation exists – and that the school has absolutely no spare funds to provide one.'

'There is, I believe, a stable block?' Lady Arabella inquired innocently. 'Unused?'

George hesitated a wary half second before nodding consent.

'Yes.'

'I will pay for its conversion,' Lady Arabella went on. 'The school will then offer it to the couple on condition that they withdraw absolutely any charge against Christopher either now or at any future date.'

'You will pay?' asked George, astounded.

'Yes.'

'May I ask why?'

'Because I choose to,' Lady Arabella answered flatly, and dismissed further interrogation with a firm smile. 'Any further objection, John darling?'

'None, as long as the couple can be persuaded to agree.'

'That is where we must rely on Mr Drummond,' Lady Arabella purred.

'It's sheer bribery,' George protested.

'But that's exactly what the law is about, Mr Drummond,' Lady Arabella argued. 'It exists to bribe people to keep out of trouble. It's the same with this scruffy little school of yours. Do we have an agreement?'

'I am unused to bribery.'

'You have no sensible alternative,' Lasko advised.

'Don't let's be difficult, dear Mr Drummond,' Lady Arabella teased, but without warmth. 'I'd been told you were stuffy – Victorian principles and all that – but do try to unbutton, just a teeny bit. Join the rest of us in the second half of the twentieth century.'

'I happen to regret the passing of many of those values,' George admitted, his eyes sparking with resolve. 'By no means all, but a great many.'

'Oh, so do I, Mr Drummond,' Lady Arabella agreed, and bestowed upon George a most benevolent gaze.

The common room radio set, legacy of some long-retired master, whistled and hummed, and spluttered an unintelligible babble of voices all crackly with static, while on his knees Gunz watched the needle sweep the glowing dial, directed haphazardly across the airwaves by his unsteady hand. The orange light it cast across his face gave his fleshy features a malevolent look, and his crouching posture was eerily dwarfish.

'What are you doing, Siggy?' Charles inquired, his entry unobserved by the doctor until he spoke.

'I'm trying to get Vienna,' Gunz answered impatiently. 'The Russians are about to invade Hungary, and once into Hungary, why stop there? Straight on to Vienna!

And what does this blasted country go and do? Does it take a stand? No, it invades Egypt! Criminal idiots!'

'Are you quite sure?'

'Of course, I'm sure.' Gunz turned briefly from the radio to glare accusingly at Charles. 'Where have you been all evening, Charles? It's all over the news. The British Empire is over, finished, but these lunatics still haven't realized it! Ach!' He shook the set violently and banged it down, before clicking it off. 'Bloody machine!'

'Why did Arabella pay, Siggy?' Charles asked, as Dr Gunz wiped his flushed face with a handkerchief. 'I know I'm not supposed to know that she did, but what made her do it? For Chris, I mean.'

'She's known him since childhood,' said Gunz, shifting his attention and the action of his handkerchief to his glasses, so that he blinked myopically at Charles as he talked. 'She used to get him out of trouble then, own up to breaking the conservatory window when it was he who'd done it, that sort of thing. She got into the habit of rescuing him, that's all. If you can call it a rescue this time,' he added doubtfully.

'Isn't it?'

'I would not want to see my former mistress, who is pregnant by me, married to another man and living on my doorstep. Would you, Charles?'

Charles answered with a long face.

'Exactly,' said Gunz emphatically. 'It's bizarre, is it not? But Arabella arranges, and what Arabella arranges, then Christopher accepts.' He raised his hands to mime surrender.

'Poor Christopher,' Charles murmured.

'Indeed,' Gunz agreed, 'poor Christopher.'

*

George sat with his elbows on his desk and his face hidden behind his hands, while his fingers turned slow circles against his forehead, their pressure enough to leave pinkish blotches above each eyebrow when he sat back suddenly in his chair. He pulled the phone across the desk and dialled Mary's number.

'Mary?' he said when she answered, and smiled because she recognized his voice. 'I've had a hell of a bloody awful day, but it has just occurred to me that all may not be irretrievably lost. Is that film still on? If it is, perhaps we could see it tonight.'

There was a pause at the other end of the line, then Mary said, 'Didn't Charles tell you?'

'Charles?' George asked, surprised. 'Tell me what?'

'We went to see it while you were in London at your emergency meeting.'

'No,' George replied quietly, 'he didn't tell me.'

'He probably forgot.'

'Was it good?'

'Very.'

'Well,' said George. 'Another time.'

'That would be lovely.'

'I'd better get back to my books.' George left a space, but Mary said nothing. 'Goodbye.' He heard Mary say goodbye and replaced the receiver.

His hand still hung there listlessly when the phone rang, and he snatched the handset spontaneously to his ear.

'Drummond.'

Mary's voice said, 'There are other films on, you know. Shall I get the paper and see?'

7

The news of Binny's breakdown had spread rapidly through the school, embroidered more and more outlandishly as it was passed from boy to boy, until in even the most subdued versions he was pictured fleeing naked across the playing fields spouting scriptures. In the staff common rooms it had been accompanied, not unnaturally, by speculation about his imminent dismissal, prompting Susan's plea for leniency from the headmaster, an intervention which, in fact, influenced George's decision to grant Binny a reprieve until the end of term, when his case would be reconsidered, less than Sir Foster Gill's unwavering support for his appointee.

While his colleagues were less openly aggressive than they had been before Binny's 'incident', more often than not his invitations to take a turn around the school grounds before retiring were turned down, books and newspapers were picked up and pored over at his entry, and doors were closed bluntly behind his back. Binny was oblivious to much of this unfriendliness, however, and he himself was confident enough of his rehabilitation to ask to spend the impending Christmas holidays *en famille* with the headmaster's household, though Charles, to whom the proposal was made, neglected to mention it to his father.

Fortified by the four absolutes of Moral Rearmament

– absolute unselfishness, absolute purity, absolute love and absolute honesty – which he litanized every time he washed or shaved or combed his hair or tweaked his tie straight in the mirror where four adhesive circles announced them, Binny soldiered on. His ceaseless crusade to ignite a spiritual fire in the school caused him to twitch with anticipation as the staff assembled in the men's common room to appraise the end of term reports.

'I'd been enjoying a degree of complacency on the evidence of these reports,' George began, when each of his teachers had found a space in which to settle, and he patted a stack of papers beside him, 'until Siggy ruined it all. He tells me a good school report is rarely a report on the boys, but merely self-congratulation on the teacher's part.'

'Oh, well done, Siggy,' Charles commented above a chorus of groans.

'Well?' asked George, carrying his inquiry to every teacher in the room with a sweeping circular look. 'The majority of these reports are excellent. Nothing wrong with them at all. But Siggy has made me wonder.'

'The theory is interesting, but fanciful,' said Fordham, 'and, of course, quite slanderous.'

'I have no wish to throw stones,' Gunz said defensively. 'I myself may not be entirely blameless, but the intellectual air of the school has grown stale.' His colleagues stared at him, Binny's eyes burning brightest.

'But when did you ever find it bracing, Siggy?' Charles demanded with a laugh that was cut short by his father's frown.

'What I'd appreciate,' George said, 'is a frank report on the state of the nation from your several points of view.'

'There is also a habit of ill-discipline creeping into the senior classes,' Gunz observed.

'Haven't you got a bit of a bee in your bonnet about the senior classes, Siggy?' George suggested, then added after a moment's consideration, 'But yes, all right, a poor performance there is the last thing we want. It hits our reputation where it hurts – in the bank balance.' He glanced from Gunz to the others. 'Do the senior boys get enough exercise, do you think?'

'Senior boys never get enough exercise,' Heritage answered flatly.

'If I can stick my oar in here,' said Braithwaite, rising from his seat to add weight to his words. 'On discipline' – his stance and stern face suggested a practical demonstration might be about to take place – 'I'll be frank, none of you young chaps knows how to use his voice. The teacher's voice is his number one weapon. With the right tone and the right sort of projection you can pin twenty bloodthirsty hooligans to their desks with a word. A name can be enough. One boy's name tossed like a hand-grenade into the eye of the storm produces instant hush. Parker, for instance. We're all acquainted with him, are we not?' He acknowledged groans and nods around the room with a nod of his own, and barked, 'Parker! Try it, practise it in front of a mirror. You'll scare yourselves silly, I assure you. Mock if you like,' he warned, when several masters smiled and one or two even laughed at the suggestion, 'but I've been in places and seen boys that would turn your blood cold, and I've never had any trouble.' With a last authoritarian look he sat down again.

'Thank you, Bertie,' George said with a smile which flickered between gratitude and amusement. 'I'm sure that's excellent advice.'

Binny's distinctive prefatory hum attracted the

attention of the assembly before George could continue.

'The major's advice is perfectly adequate so far as it goes,' Binny said, then shook his head disconsolately, 'but have you never noticed how in this world for every thousand hacking at the branches of evil only one will be found attacking the root?'

'What is it you want to say, Tim?' George asked doubtfully.

'Dr Gunz mentions "staleness" – that's interesting. This very afternoon when I returned to school from an invigorating outing I too was struck by the staleness, and there's no doubt in my mind what's causing it.' He looked emphatically from face to face. 'This school is spiritually dead.'

'Don't take Bertie's hooligans too literally, Tim,' George told him. 'What we've got here is a houseful of small boys in short trousers learning the rules of the game.'

'But is that really all we want to give them? The rules of the game? Where are their spiritual values? What are they taught to value in and for itself?'

Fordham rose huffily to his feet.

'If you'll excuse me, headmaster. My night on the dorms.'

George gestured his assent and watched Fordham depart, before turning back to Binny with evident irritation.

'Come on, Tim. Let's not have that "Others before self, God before all", please. Our philosophy on games is play for the sake of playing. You don't have to win, but you must do your best.'

'Shrewd, I grant you, very shrewd,' said Binny, then wagged his finger. 'But not quite good enough.'

'Well, perhaps you'd like to improve on our efforts, then?' George suggested drily.

'God willing, Headmaster, God willing,' Binny declared, his voice and his broad smile radiating a confidence that was not reflected in the faces of his listeners.

Binny's missionary fervour would not subside. In the chapel and in the classroom he fought the good fight of faith, and conducted in the cause of his campaign a survey of the boys' biblical knowledge, confronting George subsequently with the results.

'You were right, of course, Headmaster,' he said, as George, head in hands, gazed unhappily at the sheets of juvenile scrawl spread in front of him on the desk.

'I?' asked George, taken aback. 'What did I have to do with it?'

'It was your suggestion that I should try to improve the boys' spiritual education.'

'So it was,' sighed George.

'And these essays,' Binny went on, 'are perfect proof that I hadn't been doing my job properly.' He sifted through the papers, selected one, and read aloud: '"Christmas means Father of God who sent his baby Jesus down the chimney to Mary which is why we hang our stockings on the chimney-piece to catch him only I never have."' He replaced the sheet squarely in front of George. 'Oh, and I asked Forbes in 2B to write out the Lord's Prayer, and he began, "Our Father which art in Heaven, Harold be thy name."'

George allowed a smile to show.

'They're very young, Tim.'

'That's partly it, Headmaster,' Binny agreed enthusiastically. 'I can see now what a fool I've been. My idea for a Bible-reading club was on absolutely the wrong lines. No good at all for such active young chaps, but this is where my new scheme comes in.' He reached inside his jacket and pulled out a piece of paper, which he unfolded and handed to George. 'My own sketch, sir,' he explained, as George looked up dubiously. 'The boy's not very good, but it gives an idea of the sort of uniform I have in mind.'

George continued to eye him attentively, and Binny hurried on, 'What I'd like to do is to set up a group of lively-minded imaginative boys into a kind of ginger group, if you like, a network of God's agents with a boy in each class – I've got my eye on one or two already – and a boy in each dorm, always vigilant, always available, quietly spreading the Word about our Lord, privileged to wear special uniform, with weekly meetings and special responsibilities in the community. I shall call the group the Apostles.'

While Binny paused for breath, George said steadily, 'Tim, I'm sorry, but that sort of thing is quite out of the question.'

Binny reeled slightly, as if George's response bore a physical force.

'Out of the question?' he asked, blinking. 'Why's that?'

'There's just no place for that sort of thing in this school.'

'You mean there's no place for God?' Binny demanded. 'No place for a sense of mission? No place for the struggle between good and evil?'

'You're loading the question, Tim,' George replied in a voice that had lost a degree of patience. 'This isn't a seminary, it's a lay school. It's our duty to fit boys for their senior schools and for the world –'

'Is this or is this not a Christian establishment?' Binny interrupted excitably.

'Of course it is. Part of the boys' education is religious. A practising, believing Christian, i.e. you, Tim, instructs them in the Bible, and in our own small way we struggle against evil, if the sort of petty thing we come up against can really be termed evil. I'm not sure it can.'

Binny stabbed his drawing, which George had dropped on the desk, with a finger.

'What you don't appreciate, Headmaster, is the value of a uniform.'

'Oh, come on, Tim. We're all on your side, but the sort of thing you're suggesting is going way too far. The vicar will be with us this Sunday. If you're still worried, why not have a word with him? And one more thing, they're little lads we're talking about, and even the Bible can be fun, don't you think?'

Far from following his headmaster's advice to confide in the vicar, Binny did not even remain in the congregation until the end of the service, stalking indiscreetly from the chapel during the sermon, a demonstrative exit which Mary Prior recalled as she and George drank sherry afterwards in his sitting room.

'The vicar looked like a man unaccustomed to arousing such passion,' she remarked, declining a second glass by placing her palm over the rim. 'But looking on the bright side, at least Binny is showing a keen interest in his job, wouldn't you say?'

George returned the decanter to its tray and sat down.

'The last member of staff who showed that degree of interest was found drilling the boys on the lawn at five in the morning.'

'Oh Lord,' Mary laughed.

'Frankly, it was all very well for the boys, but the staff couldn't stand being woken by a dawn chorus of Latin verbs sung to the tune of "Ten Green Bottles",'

George said, and rewarded his story with a quick sip, before going on, 'but I take your point. Just a pinch more drive from the rest of them would be no bad thing. Perhaps Leo might prescribe some pep pills to liven them up a bit. Ah,' he exclaimed as Edward appeared in the doorway, 'here's your young man.'

'Hello, darling.'

Mary stood up and held out her arms, but although Edward took several steps into the room, he stopped short of the offered embrace.

'Hullo, mother. Are we going?'

'Yes, darling, of course,' Mary said, with an embarrassed glance at George. 'Patience.'

'You said we could go somewhere I liked.'

'Edward!'

'That reminds me, Mary,' said George. 'Something I meant to ask you.'

'You run along to the car, darling,' Mary told Edward, and watched him walk smartly from the room. 'He's growing up,' she said to George when he had gone. 'I'm not sure I like it.'

'Boys do,' said George, 'but there's no need to worry about Edward. Between you looking after him at home and me looking after him here, I think we'll turn him into a fine young man. You wait and see.'

'Mmmm,' Mary murmured without conviction, but added more brightly, 'what was it you were going to ask me?'

'I have to go into town next Friday to collect some new equipment for the music room. I wondered if you'd like to join me? Have lunch? My business won't take five minutes.'

Mary bit her lip. 'Next Friday? Oh, George, I'm so sorry. I can't.'

'Not to worry.'

'But it's a lovely idea,' Mary was quick to reassure him with a smile. 'Another time would be delightful.'

'Another time, then. Have a nice tea – and be sure to feed him something he can make the other boys envious of when he gets back to school. I often think that's half the pleasure of their afternoons out.'

As they talked, they had followed Edward towards Mary's car, but parted before they were clear of the school buildings, Mary quickening her pace across the gravel, George turning slowly back towards his house, pausing momentarily at the window of the men's common room to scrutinize the sleeping heads inside.

Binny's was not among them, since he had recently abandoned his dozing associates, albeit unconvinced of the authenticity of every snore, and made his way moodily to the art room. His entry was greeted by what were now customary sniggers from several boys in spattered aprons, but went unnoticed by Susan until he stood directly above her at the low table where she was supervising the construction of a nativity scene from cardboard, coloured paper and paint.

'Having fun?' he asked her when she looked up with a start.

'I love it,' she said, recovering sufficiently from his unexpected arrival to smile. 'It's like being a child all over again.' She held up a cut-out figure of Mary for his inspection before positioning it by a crib made out of a matchbox. 'What do you think of our efforts?' she asked, but Binny did not answer. 'My brothers and I used to make one every year.' Binny, his face set, still made no response. 'Are you all right, Tim?'

'They've a funny idea of Christmas, you know,' Binny muttered, his voice so strangled in his throat that Susan had to strain upwards to hear.

'Who?'

'The boys,' Binny explained gruffly. 'They haven't got the first idea what it's all about.'

'Of course they have,' Susan contradicted crossly, indicating the busy fingers which were creating the other figures that would fill the stable scene. 'These ones know the story by heart. I mean, even I like the Christmas story.'

'But what Christmas story, eh?' Binny demanded in a voice loud enough to distract every boy at Susan's table and most of the others in the art room. 'Matthew tells it one way, Luke another, and tradition has added a lot of dubious trimmings along the way. All those shepherds and mangers and oxen and asses.'

'I'm surprised at your pedantry, Tim,' Susan said, pointedly picking up a pair of scissors and a square of cardboard on which a donkey was crudely outlined. 'You don't expect me to rob the story of all its colour simply to toe some stuffy academic line, do you? Surely it's the meaning that counts?'

'Naturally it's the meaning, Susan, but what does your kindergarten crib tell us about the meaning? Christmas is terrifying!'

'Tim!' said Susan sharply, but she could not prevent him hurtling breathlessly onwards, oblivious of the unrest he was causing.

'God became the lowest of the low, an illegitimate child of the poor, born in pain and blood to an all too human destiny, but yours is a fairy story, all sweetness and light, a twopenny-halfpenny romance where the baby Jesus comes into the world floating down a bloody moonbeam.'

The use of an expletive by a master was always a matter for mirth amongst the boys, and Binny's invective put the room in uproar, the laughter redoubled by the release of tension built up by that short angry speech. Susan, who had risen slowly to her feet during Binny's outburst, bustled him to the nearest door, which opened into a store cupboard.

'Come on, Tim,' she said firmly, as she shoved him into the dim, cramped stockroom which smelled of powder paint and plasticine, 'that's enough. What are you trying to do? At this age they don't even know the facts of life. So far as they're concerned, perhaps real babies come sliding down a moonbeam. Is this the way you carry on when you're in charge of a class? Is it?'

'They love it,' said Binny, his eyes shining in the gloom. But catching a look of horror on Susan's face, he added, 'Well, no, not exactly like this, but tough talk, exciting stuff all the same.' As the door swung shut behind them to silence the barrage of ridicule, his tone altered. 'I need your support, Susan,' he moaned, and sighed heavily.

'Mine?' scoffed Susan. 'But I thought you had God on your side.'

'You've changed, Susan. Lately I've noticed a hardness –'

'Nonsense!' Susan snapped, but then said more gently, 'Don't say that.'

Binny slumped on to a stack of wrapped reams of art paper, dragging Susan down with him on to his makeshift seat.

'I do miss a uniform,' he murmured.

Susan shook her head, but smiled.

'I know I'm a shocking mess,' Binny went on. 'Never did adapt to civvies, somehow, but now for the first time since I left the Navy I can see what's wanted of me. It's just not good enough, you know.'

'What isn't?'

'All this bunkum about babies and shepherds. You see, what no one remembers is that at the end of it all the shepherd sells his sheep to the market for food – lambs to the slaughter and all that.'

Susan winced as Binny began to work the hand he held between his as if he were kneading clay, but when she tried to wrest it away and stand up, he squeezed it tighter still.

'Don't go, Susan,' he begged, 'please don't go. I must have someone to believe in me.'

With her free hand Susan stroked the back of Binny's, and his grip loosened.

'Of course I believe in you, Tim, but my belief may not be enough.'

His eyes pierced the depths of hers for a painful second, then his head jerked down against her rib cage with an impact that made her gasp, while his encircling arms clamped them together in this awkward embrace. He rubbed his face against the knobbled wool of her man's pullover, breathing loudly through his nose as he did.

'Tim!' Susan hissed furiously, and she pummelled his shoulders with her fists until he let her go. As she snatched the door open, his eyes shone blindly in the wedge of light that split the dark cupboard. Binny was crying.

'The boys said you were in the store room with Binny,' Wendy said, taken aback, as she stood in the centre of the art-room floor in an attitude that indicated an attempt to impose authority. 'I thought they were pulling my leg.'

Brushing aside Wendy's astonished observation, Susan said, 'Would you mind taking this lot for five minutes? I need some fresh air.'

'I don't mind getting them to clear up.'

'Why clear up?'

'Because matron's been sounding off about their

games kit again. They've been putting their black plimsolls and their white plimsolls in the same bag, so they've got to sort them out.' Wendy shrugged as Susan rolled her eyes upwards. 'Now.'

Susan grabbed her coat from the back of the door.

'Is this whole bloody place out of its mind?' she murmured loud enough to set off another round of sniggers, which Wendy silenced with a clap of her hands.

In the dim cupboard Binny was on his knees, his hands pressed together in front of his bowed forehead.

'Hear my prayer, O Lord,' he whispered passionately, 'and let me crying come unto thee. Hide not thy face from me in the time of my trouble. For my enemies revile me all the day long and they that are mad upon me are sworn together. My days are gone like a shadow and I am withered like grass.'

8

As the troop call pierced the silence of the wintry afternoon, boys in khaki uniform broke from bushes and hedgerows and raced across the school grounds to surround Heritage who, identically dressed with the addition of a mildewed hat and patches on the elbows of a shirt which had faded to the colour of silver sand, rubbed his hands enthusiastically at their approach.

'Well done, scouters,' he bellowed so the stragglers could hear. 'Some of you had your quarry in quite a fix there – but you didn't all take in what I told you about cover. You, Davies, when will you learn just because you haven't got eyes in your rear end doesn't mean it's invisible? And remember, it's not just bushes and trees that'll conceal you – did anyone take advantage of the smoke from Sam's bonfire?'

A boy with red blotches of excitement burning on his pale cheeks shot up a hand.

'Good work, Stapleton, top marks again.' Heritage ruffled the boy's hair, tugged a burr from its tousled strands and held it up for inspection. 'See, boys, you've really got to get in amongst that cover. Mind you,' he added, examining the sleeves of Stapleton's shirt with theatrical disdain, 'I'm glad I don't have to do your laundry. Now off you all go and get changed for tea.'

The boy at Stapleton's side nudged him as they

turned towards the school. 'I bet you think you're Davy Crockett, don't you? How did you manage to vanish into thin air?'

'Fell in a ditch, if you must know, Jackson,' Stapleton said with a grin. 'Right on top of a whopping great dead rat.'

'Pull the other one,' sneered the other boy. 'It's got bells on.'

'Cross my heart and hope to die,' Stapleton insisted. 'It was about two feet long with great big yellow teeth. Old Sam says they run up your trousers.'

'Ugh!' Jackson grunted, and shuddered.

'He had string tied round his ankles to stop them running up his legs.'

'But you only had shorts on.'

Stapleton grimaced and grabbed handfuls of material from each leg of his shorts until they were tight around his thighs. Both boys studied this solution and laughed.

'Seeing as you're so awfully good at tracking, Stapleton,' Jackson teased, sounding the name in an approximation of Heritage's catarrhal tone, 'why don't you sneak up on old Blubbins and slip a kipper in his coat pocket when he's out preaching to the trees?'

They stopped to watch Binny stride across the lawn and disappear into the drifting shroud of smoke from Sam's bonfire. Stapleton grinned at Jackson.

'Easy-peasy,' he said. 'But couldn't it just be a conker?'

The vicar's wife stopped whistling to herself and pronged the garden fork into the heavy soil when she noticed Binny leaning on the gate, snorting small clouds from his nostrils.

'It must be a great comfort,' he said with envy in his

voice, 'a garden. I've never had one myself, but I can see it must be a great comfort.'

'Oh, it is, it is – "one is nearer to God's heart" and all that. There's no need for talk in a garden.'

'I must see the vicar,' Binny said, reaching for the latch.

'Oh dear, I'm sorry, you can't. He's most frightfully busy. Why don't you call back tomorrow?'

'I can't,' said Binny desperately. 'I have to see him now.'

The vicar's wife looked from Binny to the house and back to Binny, then took off her gardening gloves.

'Very well,' she said with a sigh. 'I'll tell him you're here. Commander Binny, isn't it?'

Binny followed her round to the back of the vicarage and wiped his feet with unnecessary thoroughness, while he waited to be admitted to the kitchen.

'Don't mind me, Vicar,' he said, once inside, and the vicar obligingly gave him the most fleeting of glances as he pounded pink fishy flesh with a heavy pestle. 'You just go ahead. Culinary skills, eh?' he went on admiringly after a moment's contemplation. 'Would you believe I have no talents?'

'Oh, I'm quite sure . . .' the vicar began vaguely, without taking his eyes off the contents of his mortar.

'None at all,' said Binny flatly. 'A little drawing, perhaps, but nothing to write home about. They say everyone has a talent, don't they? Well, in forty-seven years I've failed to find mine.'

'You probably haven't looked hard enough,' suggested the vicar, and cracked an egg expertly against the mortar's rim. 'You never know, you might have a talent for tap-dancing or playing the harp, and I bet you haven't tried either.' He cracked a second egg single-handedly and looked at Binny, who was himself looking for a button which had fallen from his jacket and rolled under the table.

'My father, on the other hand,' Binny continued, when he stood up, flushed from his search, 'now there was a talented man. He was a cartographer by trade, and a keen amateur tennis player.' Binny saw the vicar was now reading a recipe book. 'I hope I'm not boring you.'

'Not at all,' said the vicar absently, 'not at all.'

'An ordinary man, or so he seemed, but every evening and on Sunday afternoons from March till October, my father was a faith healer.' Binny's heels clicked on the tiled floor as he began to pace about animatedly. 'In some circles he was a famous man – a man who inspired awe and, of course, faith. But you know, a very strange thing happened. I had a shocking stammer as a boy, perfectly shocking, and my poor father completely failed to cure it. But the day he died, my stutter vanished. What do you say to that, Vicar?'

'Extraordinary,' the vicar observed, as he spooned the mixture into a sieve. 'Perhaps subconsciously you felt liberated.'

'Not subconsciously at all,' Binny said emphatically. 'On the contrary, conscious as could be. You see, I'd been brought up to feel it was my fault. It wasn't my father's fault, it was mine. I'd been brought up to see pain and evil and suffering were all illusions, and to experience them was some kind of damned failure. Do you see?' The vicar looked up hurriedly and nodded. 'But, the day my father died I realized he was a charlatan.'

'How was that?'

'He committed suicide.'

'Oh, dear.'

The vicar rested the sieve on the mortar and looked at Binny with concern, but Binny gave an abrupt laugh.

'As you say, vicar, oh, dear! A faith healer who couldn't heal his own son and a cuckolded husband who killed himself! Not too good at all, eh? Left a chap feeling pretty let down, I can tell you.'

'What a terrible experience, Commander,' said the vicar, oozing unction. 'But this was all some time ago, surely?'

'The long and the short of it was that I had been deceived. Suffering wasn't an illusion, but it took me years to see it isn't the whole of life either. To see that where it doesn't actually kill off, it can enrich.' Binny broke off and leaned across the kitchen table. 'In saying this, I am, of course, teaching my grandmother to suck eggs.'

The vicar picked up the sieve and began to strain the mixture with pressure from the back of the spoon.

'You flatter me.'

Binny leaned closer. 'I know I do,' he said, and bared his teeth in a humourless grin as the vicar stiffened. 'I can't pretend it hasn't occurred to me to wonder how many have been lost to God because of the sentimentality of his ministers.' The vicar stepped back defensively, grasping the sieve like a shield and the wooden spoon like a sword, but Binny's voice boomed on. 'I wonder how many have found it impossible to believe in your bloodless Christ. Is it surprising that the churches are full of choir boys and old women?'

This last angry eruption brought the vicar's wife in from the garden.

'Is everything all right, John?'

'Perfectly, dear,' he said, eyeing Binny apprehensively, 'though I'm not sure how good my quenelles are going to be.'

His wife and Binny laughed, she nervously, he with derision.

'An interesting talk, Commander,' said the vicar, encouraged by his wife's appearance, 'but its urgency escapes me.'

'I'm simply asking you,' Binny began more reasonably than before, 'to remember your responsibility to the boys, to remember that it's in your power to throw open the windows of their souls – or to close them for ever.'

'We both have onerous responsibilities, Commander, and I do understand, of course, that a schoolmaster's life is a lonely one.'

'No, no,' said Binny, growing animated again, 'it's not that. You see, I was let down badly, and I don't want the same thing to happen to our young charges at Drummonds. What I'm trying to say is, don't fill their heads with biblical fairy tales, because it's just not fair.'

'Do you pray?' the vicar asked.

'Of course I pray, vicar,' Binny retorted angrily.

'Good,' said the vicar, while Binny's eyes blazed. 'And on a more worldly level, might I urge you to take greater care of yourself? Plenty of fresh air and perhaps a new interest? You never know,' he added, working his spoon into the mixture again, 'you might find you have a talent for fishing.'

That suggestion seeped through Binny's mind like the mousse through the vicar's sieve, as he pounded the path back to school. 'Fishing,' he muttered, 'fishing,' again and again, turning the word over in his head so many times that it disintegrated into a meaningless mishmash of sound.

'I am become like a pelican in the wilderness,' he shouted into the wind, 'and like an owl in the desert, for mine enemies revile me all the day long.'

Suddenly he stopped in his tracks and stared hard into the evening sky, as if he was focusing on a distant light. 'Fishing,' he said carefully, enunciating the word with awe.

'Follow me' – his voice roared like rolling thunder – 'and I will make you fishers of men.'

Stapleton patted his pocket to check that the conker, a horse-chestnut selected by Jackson with the sheen of a new brown shoe and almost the size of a toe-cap, had not fallen out as he dodged between the gravestones in the deserted churchyard. He crouched in the porch until Binny's footsteps stopped ringing on the flagged floor of the nave and then swung the heavy door just wide enough to allow him to slip in sideways. As he crawled cautiously along the narrow aisle between the rows of pews and the wall, he could hear Binny singing in the vestry, and he was about to chance a dash to the shadow of the pulpit, when Binny emerged, dressed in a white surplice. He froze, as Heritage had taught him, not daring to breathe for a full half minute, while Binny scanned the silent church, before dropping to his hands and knees, apparently satisfied that he was alone.

From his hiding place Stapleton could hear the rustle of Binny's skirts and his grunts and mutters, but an irresistible curiosity to discover his precise activity led him to crawl into the space between two pews and inch his way patiently towards the central aisle. There he poked his head out slowly, but withdrew it immediately, for Binny's head was no more than ten feet away and the same height as his from the floor; Stapleton retreated a couple of feet and peered over the back of the pew instead.

Using his outstretched arms as a guide, Binny

appeared to be taking rough measurements of various dimensions, such as the width of the aisle, the gap between the rows of pews and between the front pew and the pulpit, noting them with a stump of pencil on the back of an envelope, then, pushing himself to his feet, he counted aloud his paces to the chancel. He spun so rapidly on his heels that Stapleton had no time to duck his head.

'Hey, you!' Binny shouted, the power of his voice in the empty nave paralysing the boy. 'Come out of there!' He strode forward and grabbed Stapleton roughly by the shoulder, dragging him into the faint patch of mottled light cast by the stained-glass window above the altar.

'Stapleton!'

'Yes, sir,' Stapleton replied glumly.

'What do you think you're doing here, boy? Shouldn't you be writing to your parents or daubing with paints or reading improving literature?'

Stapleton stayed silent, but surveyed Binny's outfit with an exaggeratedly appraising eye. Binny laughed awkwardly and made a show of brushing dust from his skirts, before pulling the surplice over his head.

'Don't want to get my trousers dirty, do I, eh?' he remarked with an attempt at carelessness. 'Always been a bit of a mucky blighter – can't seem to keep myself clean. But not a word of this, eh?'

Stapleton dissolved Binny's clandestine smile with an expressionless stare.

'Better not mention this to anyone, there's a good lad. It's a secret, you see, all in the nature of a Christmas surprise – something to make our carol service especially memorable this year. Understand?'

Stapleton nodded. 'What's it worth, sir?'

'I don't follow you, Stapleton.'

'Is it worth seven and six, sir?'

Binny groaned and sank to the chancel steps.

'Are you all right, sir?' Stapleton inquired archly.

Binny's hand flapped against the stone step beside him. 'Sit down, Stapleton.' The boy obeyed, and Binny shook his head despairingly. 'I can't believe what I just heard. All in the name of mammon! It's not your fault, Stapleton, it's the adult world that's let you down, I know that, oh how I know that. You care for nothing but success, status and power.' Seeing the boy's puzzled expression, Binny explained, 'That, I am assured, is what the school is supposed to educate you for. Success is what the teachers want and success is what your parents want, so naturally you boys think you want it too.' With a sweep of his arm, intended to draw Stapleton's attention away from secular thoughts to the church, he continued, 'Forgetting so much and so much – so much that's good, so much that's bad.' He shook his head several more times. 'In church yesterday, were you?'

'Yes, sir.'

'What did you think of the sermon?'

Stapleton shrugged uncertainly.

'I've given the man a second chance, but he's a complete wash-out. D'you hear that, Stapleton? What is he?'

'A wash-out, sir?' Stapleton said helpfully.

After a moment's reflection, Binny went on, 'Has it ever occurred to you that perhaps God isn't just good? What I mean to say is, does the good Shepherd, gentle Jesus meek and mild' – his voice had lapsed into a mocking singsong – 'does that fully express your idea of God, eh? Because I'm bound to say it doesn't express mine. No, Stapleton, I've come to see God is everything – good and bad.' The boy shuddered at his side, and

Binny remarked heartily, 'It's your education that's to blame for not preparing you for such ideas. It omits birth and death, pain and bliss, failures and miracles . . . miracles.' He slapped Stapleton's knee as he repeated the word, and said, 'Now, there's a thing. How would you like to take part in a real, live miracle, my boy? How would you like – I'm not sure how best to put this . . .' As Binny searched the vaulted ceiling for an appropriate form of expression, Stapleton transferred the conker from his own pocket into Binny's. 'How would you like to assist me in the performance of a good old-fashioned miracle? What do you think? Scared, eh?' he asked, when the boy blinked at him. 'Is that it?'

'No, sir, it's not that at all. I'd like to very much, but –'

'No buts, Stapleton,' Binny said, and cuffed the back of his head playfully. 'The fact is that even God needs a helping hand at times. But,' he warned, putting a finger to his lips, 'not a word to anyone. Not a word.'

'Did someone mention Christmas?' Heritage inquired gloomily, eyeing the struggling fire in the common room grate rather than any one of his fellow masters who were trying to derive warmth from the newly stacked, smoking coals.

'I certainly didn't,' replied Fordham. 'The word never passes my lips.'

'What I mean is,' Heritage continued in the same despondent tone, but with a half-hearted gesture at the unadorned walls, 'there's precious little sign of it in here.'

'Craving a little tinsel, are we?' Fordham asked sourly. 'Or perhaps some coloured baubles from a

Woolworth's counter and a nice bunch of mistletoe?'

'Yes, damn you, Chris! Why the hell not?'

'I think we can do rather better than that, in fact, Patrick,' said Braithwaite, lowering his newspaper an inch. 'The lovely Lady Arabella is sending the staff of Drummonds her seasonal greetings – and a crate of champagne.'

'Good Lord!'

'Can this be true, Siggy?' Fordham asked.

'Yes,' Gunz conceded reluctantly, 'actually she is.'

'A girl worth her weight in gold,' Braithwaite observed.

'I take it you mean that literally, Bertie?' said Fordham.

'Champagne!' Heritage savoured the word with a satisfied smack of the lips. 'It's the very thing we all need.'

'I'm not so sure about all of us,' Fordham protested drily. 'Frankly, I don't think Binny should be offered any fizz.'

'Quite right,' agreed Heritage. 'The man's wound up enough already. Isn't it time our headmaster did something about him?'

'He's been conducting a discreet opinion poll,' Braithwaite said. 'Hasn't he spoken to you, yet?'

'Yes, but that's not the same as doing something about him. I can't understand why he hasn't hauled him up.'

'Probably because he's giving the poor old sod enough rope to hang himself with first,' suggested Charles.

'Shouldn't be difficult,' said Fordham. 'But if he fluffs it, I'll give him a hand with the knots.'

'I don't know what you're all bleating about,'

Braithwaite remonstrated, folding his paper emphatically on his lap. 'A few weeks ago the chap did nothing but sit around sobbing. Now he's as happy as a sandboy.'

'But he's such an excessively boisterous sandboy, Bertie,' Fordham argued. 'At least he used to sob quietly.'

'Are you suggesting we should be seriously worried about him, Christopher?' asked Gunz.

Fordham wrinkled his nose to convey an effort of deep thought, then shrugged.

'I don't really think there's much wrong with Binny that a devoted woman and a trip to the dry cleaner's wouldn't put right.'

Even before the laughter subsided, Binny was forgotten, along with his absences, his eccentric hours, his smug smiles and his ebullience as unshakable as his air of secrecy, for he and his extraordinary ways comprised a less stimulating subject for public debate and private pondering than one dozen bottles of Lady Arabella's bubbly.

As the vicar moved to climb the pulpit stairs, Stapleton slipped from his pew, unnoticed by all but the boy beside him, whose eyes Stapleton redirected to the altar with a glower and a raised fist. He stole along the shadowy east wall and through a door behind the choir.

The vicar studied the congregation of blazered boys, masters in gowns and parents in their Sunday smartest, with a benedictory smile.

'Dearly beloved, rejoice in the Lord always, and again I say, rejoice. Let your moderation be known unto all men, the Lord is at hand. Be careful for nothing, but in everything, by prayer and supplication, let your requests be made unto God. And the peace of God that passes all understanding –'

The soporific drone was interrupted by an explosion that appeared to erupt from the chancel ceiling, followed almost immediately by another. Their thunderous reverberations sent heads ducking down behind the pews, some with palms pressed hard against ears to dampen the din, others in anxious prayer. A third deafening boom, which emanated from a flash, bright enough to leave an image on the eyeballs of those who saw it, in the air above the pulpit, brought men with military minds to their feet, but the vicar, gripping the pulpit rail with the white knuckles of one clinging to life itself, dropped to his knees, as a more devastating roar from below rocked the pulpit, dislodging the heavy Bible from the lectern. With a crash the pulpit half capsized, settling at the crazy angle of a ship wrecked on a rock, an impression which was made more vivid by the similarity of the vicar's apparently lifeless form to that of a drowned sailor.

From the spreading screen of sulphurous smoke a purple-robed figure appeared, arms held high, as prophets used to be depicted in illustrated scripture books.

'In as much as the Lord thy God is displeased with thee, his servant, the Reverend John Cummins,' the apparition bellowed in a voice whose stridency soared above the continuing eruptions, 'He has let fall thunderbolts from heaven and set consternation among the faint-hearted. For the Lord thy God is a jealous God and lo! in the terrible hour of his vengeance the self-satisfied and the worldly will cry "Mercy" in vain!'

'It's Binny,' Heritage shouted from the back of the nave.

'Verily there shall be signs in the sun, and in the moon, and in the stars, and upon the earth distress of nations, with perplexity, the sea and the waves roaring. Men's hearts failing them for fear –'

The warning voice became a roar of helpless anger as Braithwaite and Charles wrestled Binny to the ground. For a few seconds he struggled against their smothering hold, then fell limp in their arms.

Dr Hull snapped his bag shut and watched Wendy pull the bedclothes up to Binny's chin, which moved minutely as his mouth uttered inaudible sounds, before signalling to George to accompany him into the corridor.

'I think he honestly believed he had a mission, you know,' the doctor said, when they were outside. 'It seems he had visions.'

'The sad thing is, I've been waiting for a chance to get rid of him.'

'Well, this is it. He'll need long-term hospitalization. Any relatives?' he asked.

George shook his head. 'Apparently not.'

Charles appeared from the staircase and tiptoed towards them.

'That's the last of them gone, father. I don't think we've lost any.'

'No,' said George, relieved. 'I think you're right. No one threw anything at us, nobody hurled abuse or demanded their money back, did they? Touch wood, they'll all be back next term.'

'Even Peter Stapleton?'

'He seemed perfectly all right. He was clearly shaken up about Binny at first, but after he'd had a cup of tea he was quite happy to explain how Binny mined the pulpit and what fun it was letting off the bangers. Frankly, it was hard to know how to react – I mean, anger or sympathy? After all, he was only giving a hand to a member of staff.'

'True enough,' Dr Hull said with a smile.

'Amen,' said Charles.

9

Charles sat in an armchair which was turned to face the fire, one foot propped on the other knee and an old photograph album resting in the crook of his raised leg.

'Look at these, father,' he said without looking up, when he heard George enter the sitting room. Getting no response he craned his head above the back of the chair and repeated louder, 'Father?'

George smiled distractedly and came over to him, leaning his forearms on the antimacassar.

'Shoreham 1933,' Charles said, pointing out a caption. 'I suppose the pudding in the sun hat's me, is it?'

'Of course.' George's voice was as vague as his smile.

'What have you been up to?' Charles asked, and twisted his head to see his father's face.

'Oh, just poking about,' George sighed. 'I must say, it's a rum old place with no one in it.'

'What about this one?' said Charles, indicating another photograph.

'Our wedding – August 1929.'

Charles examined the photograph.

'Didn't you get married in church?'

'What made you think that?'

'I just assumed it, I suppose.'

George moved away to the window, switching on a standard lamp as he passed, and drew the curtains.

'Your mother was an atheist in those days – and a socialist, of sorts.'

Charles leaned over the arm of the chair, grinned at his father, and said, 'You're kidding! What happened?'

'She married me.'

George tested the temperature of a teapot Charles had left on the table with his hand and lifted the pot to offer his son a cup. Charles nodded. 'Please.'

'And she lived the stuffy life of a headmaster's wife,' George went on, while he poured.

'You don't blame yourself, do you, father? What's so damned stuffy about being a headmaster's wife, anyway?'

'I don't know, Charles. I suppose it's like everything else in life – it all depends.'

Charles took the cup his father handed him.

'On what?'

'On what you make of it.' George leaned over to look at the photograph. 'Ah, yes,' he said in a distant voice, 'she was pretty.' He stared silently over Charles' shoulder, then, seeing him glance at his watch, asked, 'Going out again?'

'Er, yes,' Charles answered cautiously.

'Where were you earlier? I needed a hand with the apparatus in the gym – it's time it was revarnished.'

'Why don't you get Andy to do it?'

'He's got more than enough to do outside, which is why I needed you. Where were you?'

Charles stood up, and took his tea to the mantelpiece.

'I called in on Mary,' he said carelessly. 'Thought she might find use for a man about the house.'

'What makes you think she hasn't got one?'

'You mean the queer who was there at Christmas?'
George frowned, tempting Charles to laugh.

'Really, father, you are obtuse at times. Phillip Bennett's a homosexual – nothing for you to worry about.'

'Charles!'

'Anyway, I was right,' Charles continued confidently. 'Mary was very glad to be given a hand. In fact, she was sufficiently grateful to invite me for dinner this evening.'

George put down his cup and came to face his son across the fireplace.

'Apart from the fact that you're not pulling your weight around here, Charles, I don't think it's a good idea for you to be constantly calling on Mary,' he said firmly.

'It's only the third time,' Charles protested.

'I hardly need to point out that Mary is in a very vulnerable position.'

'She's a grown woman, for heaven's sake, father, and an experienced one,' he added riskily.

'It's like a red rag to a bull, isn't it?' George said with a derisive shake of his head.

'You're wrong, absolutely wrong. If you're worried about me treating Mary badly, if that's what it is, then don't, because I shan't. The way I feel about her is different.'

'Oh?' George said coolly.

'Utterly and entirely different – I've never felt this way before.' Charles stared hard at his father, then said indignantly, 'You don't believe me, do you?'

'Of course I don't believe you, Charles. What possible reason could I have for believing you? Don't forget, I've had the pleasure of knowing you since long before you learned to pretend. I know the real, careless, greedy you. The you that used to keep me awake at night, because I thought you'd never develop any spine, any real substance.'

'All right,' said Charles defiantly, 'spit it out, why don't you? You don't want me to go anywhere near Mary, do you? Why not tell me why?'

'Because there's a bloody great sign hanging round her neck that says: "Don't touch!" Which is the very reason you can't wait to get your nasty, grubby little paws on her.'

'*I* can't wait? That's a good one. Okay, I don't mind admitting it, but I've seen the way you look at her, and that's what this is really all about, isn't it, eh?'

'You know so little, Charles,' George said wearily.

'Meaning you know it all, I suppose?'

'Meaning maturity counts for something.'

'As a matter of fact, I'm beginning to appreciate maturity myself, but let's face it, father, it's not the only thing that counts. So be realistic, why don't you? I mean, don't come stumbling out of the Ice Age straight into cloud-cuckoo-land.'

George lunged at Charles, grabbed a fistful of shirt and tie just below his throat, and spun him sideways so his back slammed against the mantel; he half raised his other hand, breathing heavily.

'It must be fifteen years since I lifted a hand to you, old boy, but if I hear a breath of scandal attaching your name to Mary's, you'll have me to answer to, so help me God!'

He let go his hold and Charles angrily smoothed his crumpled clothes.

'I look forward to it!' he snapped, and slammed the door as he strode from the room, leaving his father feeling frustrated, absurd, and as uncertain of the true cause of his violent outburst as he was, suddenly and despite himself, about what Mary might really feel – or indeed about his own feelings.

A bath, a shave, a fresh shirt, a large scotch, and several cigarettes, their smoke sucked hard into his chest, not to mention the pleasant prospect of the evening ahead, combined to restore Charles' buoyant mood by the time he arrived at Mary's, and the effects of an excellent meal improved even on that. As he sat on the sofa, the remains of an unevenly shared bottle of burgundy swirling slowly in his glass, his spirits were positively soaring.

'I was thinking on the way over, we really know nothing about you. We don't know where you're from, for instance, or what your maiden name was, where you went to school, what you did before you got married – '

'You don't even know my glove size, I suppose,' Mary interrupted. 'Why should you know any of those things?'

'I don't mean we should,' Charles submitted. 'I'm only saying we don't.'

'You know that sort of information about other boys' mothers, do you?'

Charles made a face.

'I wouldn't want to, thank you very much.'

'Now you can't get away with that sort of childishness with me, Charles,' Mary scolded.

Charles put a hand on his heart, and muttered humbly, 'Though I be poor, I'm honest.'

Mary laughed. 'Nonsense! You were brought up to lie very nicely, like the rest of us, thank heaven. And thank dear George. And thank your mother. Tell me about your mother,' she asked.

'I'm afraid when she died I was even more genuinely childish than I am now. I never really saw her as a person.' Charles hesitated, then went on, 'But I can tell you my father's still obsessed with her. It's strange, it's something I've only just realized, that she was a very pretty woman and he was in love with her – really in love, I mean. That might make me sound thoroughly moronic, but you probably know what I mean.'

'I do.'

Charles tutted. 'Parents! But it isn't just that we don't know the facts which makes you mysterious, Mary, it's a quality you have.' He narrowed his eyes in appraisal, this show of expertise undermined by a boyish grin. 'I think it's to do with the shape of your nose.'

'Mysterious?' said Mary, arching an eyebrow. 'Hardly a quality to last.'

'I'm sure you're wrong.'

'The voice of experience?' she teased.

'Well, then?'

'What?'

'Facts,' Charles demanded firmly.

'If you insist,' Mary agreed, with a show of reluctance. 'Maiden name, Spence. Born, King's Lynn, 1922.' She watched Charles' eyes flicker in an effort of mental arithmetic, and said, 'That's right – thirty-four. My father was a dentist, which resulted in a temporary phobia about being touched by him, because I couldn't stand the thought of all those mouths he'd had his fingers in.' She checked herself. 'But this isn't very fascinating at all.'

'It is,' insisted Charles. 'It's the most fascinating thing I ever heard.'

'Well,' Mary paused before resuming her story, 'a few months after I'd left school, war broke out. Then in

'41, I think it was, I got a job in a village school. It was the happiest time of my life.' The memory brought a faint smile to her mouth. 'In summer, we'd lock up the grim old school and go out into the fields to help with the haymaking, and we'd lie on the haystacks eating cheese sandwiches with home-made pickle that took the roof off your mouth.'

'The happiest time?' Charles asked, surprised. 'Happier than when you were married?'

'Oh, much, much happier,' Mary laughed, but stopped herself with a shake of her head. 'Anyway, all good things come to an end. When the war was over, I eventually went up to London and worked in a gallery in Bond Street.'

'Which explains your exquisite taste in art,' Charles broke in, and he scanned the paintings that lined Mary's walls with sudden interest.

She acknowledged his deduction with a smile, before continuing, 'Then in '47 I married David. It all seems such a long time ago,' she said regretfully. 'When Edward was born we moved into a pretty little house in Barnes. I thought of having more babies, but none turned up. Then David was killed in a car crash – that was in 1951. It was on the A40 near Cheltenham at three in the morning. The car went off the road. David was perfectly sober.' Mary paused. 'Facts – do they help?'

'Yes, and no,' Charles replied sympathetically. 'So you've been alone for five years?'

'I don't know what makes you assume that,' Mary remarked coolly. 'Well, is there anything else you want to know?'

'Everything,' said Charles, and stared into his glass of wine. 'Tell me to shut up if you want to, but what was your husband doing near Cheltenham alone at three in the morning?'

Mary waited until Charles looked at her, then smiled, holding his eyes. 'He wasn't alone.'

Charles took a gulp from his glass.

'He was with a girlfriend,' Mary went on matter-of-factly. 'That was the first I knew of her, or rather, it was the first proof. And because of the accident, everyone else got to know about her too.'

'I'm sorry,' Charles murmured, but Mary waved away his apology.

'People – even close friends – would tell me how sorry they were, and all the time I knew that they knew. It was absurd. It was one of the reasons we moved away and came here, where we didn't know a soul.'

'It must have been sheer hell.'

'Oh, I wasn't exactly grief-stricken,' she said, but hesitated. 'Perhaps I was. It hadn't been a happy marriage, but all the same I mourned because it might have been, and mourned for all those years of muddle. But mainly what I felt was anger. God, I was half-crazy with anger! And there was nowhere to take it, nothing I could do with it – nothing that was right or fair.'

'But the girl probably meant nothing to him at all.'

'You'd know about that, wouldn't you, Charles?' Mary said harshly, then her face softened into sadness. 'I'm sorry. I'm tired.'

Charles put down his glass and knelt in front of Mary. 'I can't stand this much longer,' he muttered. 'I'm crazy about you, Mary.'

Slumped against the cushions, she smiled at him despairingly, but said nothing.

'I mean it,' he said urgently.

'And I meant I'm tired,' Mary replied. 'I'd really rather you went.'

'I don't believe you.'

'Do you really think I intended going to bed with you?'

'Do you always do what you intend?'

'No.'

'Well, then?'

Charles reached to touch her throat lightly with the back of his fingers.

'I know too much about you, Charles.'

'No, you don't,' Charles whispered.

'You're too young, for a start.'

'But I get older every day.'

'So do I.'

'Mary, Mary, Mary,' he moaned, lowering his head to her lap, but she pushed him away.

'Don't you understand?' she said, her voice throbbing with feeling. 'It would mean nothing to me, nothing at all. What you would do for me, I could do for myself. I just want you to go.'

As Charles stared at her, his face flushed, then he turned away, picked up his jacket and stood in one movement, and went to the door without looking back.

'Charles, I'm sorry. I didn't mean to be so hurtful.'

She got up and moved behind him.

'I was clumsy,' Charles said, but kept his back to her.

Mary tapped him gently on the shoulder, and he turned round.

'No.'

Looking down, Charles took her hand, turning it over in his.

'Yes, I was – clumsy and stupid.'

'I'm not some half-wild horse, you know.'

'I don't know what you are,' Charles murmured sadly.

She took her hand away and gave him a playful push.

'Go,' she said, shaping the word elaborately with her lips.

Charles caught her hand and pulled her palm against his mouth. He held it there for a moment, then let it go so delicately that he might have been releasing a butterfly, and her hand hovered where he left it as the winter night rushed in.

'You're rather more formal than your son,' Mary observed, coming into the room carrying a tea tray, which she set down on the table in front of the sofa. 'You telephone first, he just turns up on the doorstep.'

George turned from the painting he was peering at to utter a grunt of amusement.

'This is fascinating,' he said, beckoning Mary to his side and tracing a finger across the landscape on the canvas. 'Here, you see, the Way comes up here, over the ridge and past those trees there, which are just the same today, and suddenly there you are on the edge of the world with the Weald spread out below you. I've a map of just this very area – I was planning to walk it again in the spring.'

'I didn't know you knew the countryside so well, George.'

'Only because I like to walk,' he said dismissively. 'And when I walk, I like to know where I am and what it is I'm looking at. I like to walk like a camel.'

'What have camels got to do with it?'

'A camel is said to be the one animal that thinks while it walks.'

'And only when it walks?' Mary inquired with a twinkling eye.

'In my case, yes.'

After a pause, Mary said, 'Did your wife like walking too?'

'Yes,' said George, and looked again at the painting. 'She did.'

'Charles was telling me about her,' Mary explained. 'I hope you don't mind?'

'Of course not,' George said, a trifle gruffly. 'You and Charles seem to have told each other a great deal. He certainly knows more about you than I do.' Then he added apologetically, 'I'm sorry – that sounded sour.'

Mary forgave him with a smile and went over to the sofa.

'Perhaps that's because we talk more,' she suggested gently. 'Or about more things.'

'While George has only one topic of conversation,' George finished her sentence. 'Drummonds.'

'I didn't say that.'

'But it's quite true,' he sighed. 'Boring old George only talks about his school.'

'You sound extraordinarily world-weary for a headmaster who hasn't even faced the first day of term yet,' Mary remarked. 'You're obviously in need of a cup of tea.'

'It comes of being an unpaid, overworked maintenance man,' George replied, examining his hands for evidence of manual labour. 'That and listening to Braithwaite go on about filling the school with girls.' He looked up sharply. 'But then, you're all for co-education yourself, of course.'

Mary handed George a cup and said calmly, 'I'm all for boys seeing girls as people, George, and the sooner they do, the better.'

'Yes, I heard that one this afternoon,' George said with a harsh laugh. 'You should get together with Bertie.'

'I did,' said Mary, 'or, more precisely, he came to see me.' She laughed weakly. 'He seemed to think I'd be an effective ally, though I can't imagine what he expected.'

'He obviously expected you to use your undeniable powers of persuasion on the backward old fool who runs Drummonds. Well,' he added thoughtfully, 'I must say you make an impressively radical trio – you, Charles and Bertie.'

Mary looked hurt.

'You don't honestly believe I would want to interfere in the running of the school, do you?'

'No, I'm sorry, Mary, of course I don't.' George passed a hand across his forehead, and continued agitatedly, 'But when the very structure of the school is under attack, I feel I have to fight back. I'm proud of Drummonds, proud of what we've achieved. In a prep school we're given care of boys for just five years, and yet I know we shape them for fifty. Doesn't the system work? On the whole?'

'Since you ask me,' said Mary, aroused, 'no, I don't think it does. It's the system that produced my husband, for a start!'

George winced. 'I didn't have the pleasure of knowing your husband,' he said as evenly as he could.

'And Phillip Bennett.'

'You mean your friend?' George inquired pointedly.

'Yes,' Mary answered drily, 'my friend. Phillip is a homosexual – a not uncommon creation of the English boarding school system.'

'You're being absurd, Mary,' George protested angrily. 'Drummonds has produced many fine young men.'

'Yes, I know,' Mary said bitterly. 'I've seen their photographs on your study wall – innocent faces in uniform, blissfully unaware that their young lives were about to end. Oh yes, I'll grant you that, George. Schools like yours are wonderful when it comes to producing men who are good at dying. But what about life, for God's sake?'

When she finished speaking, she was white with emotion, and when George left, she fell, sobbing, along the sofa's length. She hardly noticed his car start and missed the engine cutting off a moment later. But she heard the bell, and once she had wiped her eyes and straightened her hair with her fingers and she opened the door, she threw her arms around George's neck and cried again, with happiness.

10

'A headmaster is like Caesar's wife,' George observed, as he watched Mary blot out the bleak encroaching evening behind her sitting-room curtains. 'He has to be above suspicion. All it took was that one public peck on my cheek after chapel on Sunday and the chairman of governors was on to me almost before the effect had worn off.'

'Really, George,' Mary replied, facing him with a gently sardonic smile, 'we're not children. Was it that crusty old Sir Foster Gill who insisted on being introduced to me?'

George waved away the question.

'This has nothing to do with being told off for being naughty,' he said with a trace of impatience. 'What we have or haven't done is not the issue. I know you find it absurd, but it's quite simply a question of appearances. People gossip – and gossip isn't good for the school.'

'But didn't you anticipate gossip?'

'Of course I damned well anticipated it,' George said, and began to pace about the hearthrug. 'I dreaded it! I was foolish enough to assume that you would anticipate it too.'

'And to assume I'd play along?'

'Yes.' George stopped and held Mary with his eyes as he went on, 'For the very reason you just mentioned –

because we're not children. If we haven't reached the age of discretion by now, we never will.'

'And I should have expected a discreet hole-and-corner affair, is that it?' Mary demanded.

'Mary, don't you understand that I can't ask one standard of behaviour from my staff and another from myself? I can tell you, Charles has had a grand old time throwing back in my face all the pious lectures I've given him over the years.'

'And you, George, what have you been up to all these years, apart from being discreet? You're not exactly out of practice, are you?' Mary snapped, but catching sight of George's shocked stare, raised a placatory hand and added; 'Sorry, question withdrawn.' Then, to break the uncomfortable silence that followed, she gave a little laugh, and said, 'I wasn't very kind to Charles, you know.'

'I should damned well hope not!' George retorted, still angry from her earlier remark. 'The fact of the matter, which neither of you seem to understand, is that the well-being of the school depends on me being seen to uphold certain standards. My position forces hypocrisy on me – I have no choice.'

'I wouldn't worry about it, George, you're very good at it,' Mary said, then frowned at her unkindness. 'I'm sorry. I understand perfectly well, and I do respect your commitment to the school – even envy it a little, perhaps. This morning everyone crowded around you, and your time was theirs. I know I've seen it dozens of times before, but this time I felt left out – and rather silly. The reason I dressed up was to make you happy,' she explained with a helpless shrug, 'but it seems I only succeeded in embarrassing you. And now I feel as if you're asking me to be ashamed of myself.'

'No, my darling, no,' George protested, and crossed the room to hug her. 'I adore you,' he whispered, then held her away and said carefully, 'There is an alternative to discretion, you know. We could always go public.'

'A public limited company?'

'Very, very limited,' George murmured. 'Just you and me.'

Mary studied his face, as if she was looking for something else in his solemn expression. 'Is this a proposal?' she asked finally.

'Of course it is!'

'Mmmm.' Phillip Bennett let out a murmur of appreciation and walked at once to the mantelpiece, from which he picked up a small carriage clock. 'This is new,' he said, examining it with professional efficiency. 'May I be rude and ask how much you paid for it?'

'I don't know,' Mary said, and bit mischievously on a smile. 'It was a present.'

Bennett murmured his approval again, and said enviously, 'Lucky girl! It's not only quite charming, it's also rather valuable. Do I know the generous donor?'

Mary kept him waiting, teasingly, then told him, 'George,' adding as Bennett lifted one eyebrow and gave her a sideways look, 'and I don't want to know how much it's worth.'

Bennett put the clock back on the shelf.

'I wouldn't dream of it. Mind you,' he added with an almost invisible smile, 'I'd give you a good price for it.'

'Not for sale,' Mary scolded. 'How could you think it was?'

'You know I wasn't serious, Mary, but it is a nice piece. That's what caught my eye – it's the sort of thing I'm looking for at the moment.' He paused while Mary picked up a vase and disappeared into the kitchen, but called after her. 'I'm also looking for a woman like you.'

'What can you mean?' Mary's voice came back through the open doorway.

'For the business, of course. It's going rather too well for me to manage on my own, and I need an assistant.'

'How absolutely marvellous, Phillip!' Mary called from the kitchen.

Bennett waited until she reappeared with the vase now untidily crammed with flowers, before continuing, 'To be precise, I need a trainee assistant – someone who, in a year or two, could carry a lot of the work-load, go to auctions for me, do the buying, take some informed risks.' He sketched the other duties with a vague gesture. 'I'd prefer a woman – and with your eye and your background, you'd be perfect.'

Mary set the vase on the sideboard and fussed with the flowers, then said regretfully, 'What a lovely idea. I'm flattered, I really am, but my situation's completely changed.'

'Ah,' was all Bennett said in answer.

Mary repositioned several blooms, but wrinkled her nose with dissatisfaction; then she removed a stem from the vase and held it out towards Bennett.

'Would you, Phillip?' she asked. 'You're so much better at it than me.'

Bennett nodded, took off his jacket, and accepted the flower. While he was contemplating the contents of the vase, Mary said suddenly, 'George and I are going to be married.'

'You surprise me,' Bennett replied without turning.

'I surprise myself,' Mary laughed. 'And George surprises me most of all.'

'Evidently.'

'Oh, come on, Phillip,' Mary implored, 'you're being a spoilsport. You're supposed to say "Congratulations!" and "What a lucky woman!"'

'Congratulations,' said Bennett. 'And what a lucky man.'

'But I am a lucky woman. George is the most tender, the most loving man in the world, and he needs something more than a wife. More even than a trainee assistant!' she added emphatically enough to make Bennett look at her. 'He needs a full-time partner.' She scowled at him, not entirely playfully. 'Well, I must say, you look awfully faint-hearted about it.'

Bennett shook his head. 'Not faint-hearted, Mary. Surprised, yes. Optimistic, yes. Madly protective, of course.' He smiled and leaned towards her; they exchanged kisses on both cheeks. 'Blessings, my love.' Then he gazed meaningfully around the room, and said, 'But where will you live?'

'In the school, of course. Where else?' she asked, but seeing his doubtful expression, conceded, laughing, 'Yes, all right, I'll make a few changes, but that's going to be home. And everyone's been so kind to me, Phillip, so welcoming. Those flowers are from the staff. So you see, I'm going to come out of my selfish little bolt-hole and do something useful out there in the real world.'

'Are you? And is that where you've been? And does Drummonds have much to do with the real world, I ask myself?'

'You know I worked in a school during the war?' She waited for Bennett to nod, and went on, 'We used to take time off to help in the fields, and I couldn't help noticing how the local women, the farmers' wives, how their lives were all of a piece – marriage, work, babies, all part of the same thing. If they were haymaking, well, they just took the babies along with them.' Mary reddened slightly and explained hurriedly, 'Not that I'm thinking of having more babies, I don't mean that, but when I was with David, there was so little we shared. Now I want all the bits of my life to fit together – and I do want to be useful. I want to throw away my frivolous old self and begin again.'

'And I wish you every joy, my dear.'

Mary gave him a piercing look.

'But you don't believe in it, do you?'

'I'm sure whether I believe or not makes no difference.'

'Every little helps.'

Bennett took her hand and held it tenderly.

'I believe in you, Mary, and I believe in your future, but if it comes to casting off your old self, do you really think it's possible?'

Mary was staring dreamily through a veil of cigarette smoke at a football match far beyond the window of the headmaster's study, but the sound of footsteps brought her attention back into the room and she was already turning towards the door, her face marked with the bemused frown of someone disturbed from deep thought, when Wendy said, 'Mrs Prior, hello.'

'Hello, Wendy. I don't suppose you know where the headmaster is, do you?'

'He's not in the house, I know that. I've just been up to see Charles.' She grinned in answer to Mary's inquiring look, and explained, 'Measles – he's feeling absolutely rotten. Being grown up, you know, it's much worse.'

'Oh, dear,' said Mary. 'I imagine it's worse for the

nurse, too, isn't it?' They shared a smile, then Mary's eyes clouded with concern. 'Does this mean Edward's going to be coming out in spots?'

Wendy sighed and stuck out her lower lip. 'I'm afraid it means most of the school's going to.'

Mary only had time to say 'Oh', before George came striding into his study, his eyes alight at the sight of her.

'There you are,' she said.

'Have you been looking for me?' he asked happily.

'I've got the tickets at last,' she said, but George looked vague. 'For *The Devil's Disciple* – I managed to get a pair for next Thursday.'

George hit his forehead with the heel of his hand.

'I'm sorry, Mary, but the second Thursday of every month is a complete write-off.'

Mary's shoulders rose and fell with a sigh, and she put on a cross face. 'Hell!' she groaned. 'Yes, you did tell me, but I totally forgot. They're so hard to come by, I took the first I was offered. Sorry.'

'Never mind,' he said, and slipped a comforting arm around her shoulders. 'Why don't you ask Phillip to take you? I expect Wendy's told you Charles is out of action. Now I'm just waiting for the whole school to start going down like so many spotty ninepins. Promise me you'll go?' he asked, turning her towards him and kissing the tip of her nose. When she nodded, he went on, 'Now, what about our jumble sale?'

'I'm afraid I've run away,' she confessed, as George broke away and began to search his bookshelves. 'Some perfectly ghastly woman keeps asking me to judge a baby competition. The prospect appals me, but she seems to take it for granted that I'll do it. It's as if she's made out a duty roster for me, and every time we meet she burdens me with another one.'

Wendy grinned sympathetically and remarked, 'Mrs

Drummond used to do the baby competition, didn't she?'

As George turned with a sharpish look, she blushed and seemed about to open her mouth in apology, when Mary said, 'My dear Wendy, thank goodness she's actually been mentioned. Anyone would think she was George's guilty secret.' And with a look of supplication at George, she added, 'I'm sure Nancy did the baby competition, and did it very well, but my problem is every baby looks the same to me.'

'Couldn't you get away with weighing them and choosing the biggest?' George suggested brightly. 'Like a leek competition?'

Mary laughed. 'Isn't that just the sort of thing to get me drummed out of the regiment, George?'

George winked and held up a book, this gesture evidently intended to convey not only that his search had been successful, but as a consequence that he was going, for he did so without another word, leaving Mary and Wendy with little to do but shrug helplessly behind his rapidly departing back.

Mary was reminded of the moment several days later, as she fought for George's attention with a pile of papers on his desk, when eventually he replaced the cap reluctantly on his pen and held it like a soldier surrendering his weapon.

'I thought you wanted to be useful, Mary,' he said wearily.

'Of course I want to be useful,' Mary protested, 'but I don't see how it would be useful for me to make a complete fool of myself.'

'If I thought for one moment you'd make a fool of yourself, I wouldn't have suggested Lady Phipps should approach you.'

'All right,' Mary conceded. 'I'll accept it as a

compliment – just – but the fact is, I've never taken the smallest interest in the WVS.' She paused, but George said nothing, so she went on exasperatedly, 'I have never wanted to make nettle soup or knit my own union jack.'

'Mary!' George admonished her cheerfully.

'They set my teeth on edge, playing at harvest mice.'

'You do realize,' George said calmly, 'you're being asked to be a figure-head, not a grass roots member.'

'Everything you say makes it worse,' Mary snapped.

George leaned back in his chair and gave her a bleak stare.

'I thought the problem was your lack of interest,' he explained. 'I'm only trying to point out that you won't be expected to knit or pick nettles.'

'The problem is I'm being pushed into a false position – I don't want to be figure-head to an anachronism.'

She punctuated this with a mocking laugh, and there was a blunt edge of derision in George's response. 'Well, perhaps you're the one to change all that? Use your influence to drag them kicking and screaming into 1957?' Mary looked sour, and George added disconsolately, 'Whatever that is.'

'Whatever what is?'

'1957. Now. What does it mean to be contemporary? Do any of us really reside in the here and now? Whether we like it or not, the past travels with us.'

'That may be true to a certain extent, George,' Mary said, more evenly than before, 'but you see, I'm here now – I'm supposed to be the present for you.'

'But you are, Mary,' George answered with measured emphasis, 'and the future – I know that.'

'No, George, that's not what I mean.' Mary hesitated, then said quickly, 'I don't want you to expect me to be Nancy.'

No,' George said quietly, his face sagging. 'I'm sorry.'

Mary moved behind his chair and touched his cheek with the back of her hand. 'Darling, we get so little time together.' Her sigh was transmitted to her fingertips and George took hold of them. 'Even when we're married, is bed going to be our only privacy? I can't see where our own life fits into all this.'

'This is my life, Mary. It's here with you.' George pressed her hand hard against his chest. 'I love you,' he whispered.

'I know you do,' she said, reinforcing her words with pressure from her fingertips. 'But please, darling, couldn't we have just a little time away together?'

'Away?' George groaned. 'It's impossible.'

'Why?' Mary begged him. 'I thought you once loved walking? Didn't you promise me we'd walk together to that heavenly-looking place in my painting?' She shook his shoulders. 'George?' she said urgently. 'We can't go on without some time for ourselves.'

The everyday noises of the school seemed suddenly to close in on George's study: a crescendo of cries from the playing fields and the resonant boom of the master in charge, the stop-start of a choir at practice, the rattle of running feet in the corridor, interrupted by the hectoring bellow of authority, and, conducted right into the room by way of the central-heating pipes, the interminable banging of Sykes the handyman's hammer. George held his head and shut his eyes.

'Will somebody stop that infernal racket?' he shouted, but only the hammering stopped.

Between the shining dome of his head and cheeks pink with pleasure, Braithwaite's eyes blinked while he gave his glasses a final flourish with a handkerchief, before inspecting them against the light from the study window and hooking them behind his ears with a satisfied smile. Then, as if to test the efficacy of his clean lenses, he stared hard at Sykes for a second or two, and when he spoke, in spite of his excited flush, his tone was serious.

'You are no doubt aware that our head has decided to take a few days' leave and, as you probably also know, I have been honoured by being placed in temporary charge of the school. It occurs to me that under the circumstances' – here he could no longer suppress a smile – 'some small experimentation might be in order. The boys are nice little chaps on the whole, but over-protected from the simple realities of life, and it does them no good at all.'

Sykes looked confused, but said helpfully, 'Spare the rod, sir, and you spoil the child.'

'It wasn't the rod I had in mind, Sykes, but watching you mend the washbasin in Dorm Six I was inspired. The boys' salvation, I believe, lies with do-it-yourself.' He picked up a squared sheet of paper from the desk, and went on, 'I've been sitting here flicking through the boys' timetables and they read like something out of a monastic institution in the Middle Ages. Latin, religious instruction, choir practice, French, biology, more Latin, mathematics,' he read, then dropped the timetable back on the desk. 'Small wonder they turn into fops and pansies, is it, Sykes?' he demanded.

'It beats me how they know their arses from their elbows, sir,' Sykes agreed.

After the minutest hesitation, Bertie said, 'Quite so. They need bringing down to earth, Sykes, and I think you're the man to do it. They need the world of electric sockets and tap washers opened up to them. I want them to breathe the smell of turpentine and feel the texture of freshly mixed plaster. In short, Sykes, we are to make Renaissance men of them.'

'Whatever you say, sir,' said Sykes, while Braithwaite rubbed his hands with fierce enthusiasm.

'Morning Four B,' Fordham announced breezily.

'Morning, sir,' Four B answered, less so.

'I am replacing Dr Gunz, who has been called away on an errand of mercy,' Fordham explained. 'The situation is not ideal, but I want every man here to do his very best.'

A boy at the back raised his arm. 'Please, sir,' he said, 'I say, sir – '

'Yes, Sullivan?'

'Do you actually know anything about chemistry, sir?'

Fordham turned his back on a nervous chorus of giggles and wiped the blackboard clean, before replying, 'I know quite enough to get by, Sullivan, thank you. And what's good enough for me is certainly good enough for you.'

A second hand shot up, and a voice chimed, 'It might not be, sir. I mean, what if Sullivan decided to be a chemist?'

'Dammit, Thompson,' Fordham growled. 'If Sullivan is so completely lacking in style as to consider chemistry a vocation, then be it on his own head. Now,' he said, sweeping the ranks of desks with a firm stare, 'copy out these formulae into your notebooks.'

The stub of chalk between his fingers clicked busily against the board while he wrote, and the silence when he stopped in mid-stroke brought every boy's eyes on to his back. He wheeled round angrily, his small eyes narrowing, pointed at two empty desks, and said in a voice weighed down with irony, 'I'm missing two dear, familiar little faces, am I not? Jones and Phillips,' he answered himself after a moment's consideration, the class keeping wisely quiet. 'Now, what could possibly attract them more than chemistry, I wonder?'

Fordham threw down the chalk, which bounced from the podium, and strode from the room without so much as a warning against the noise that erupted inevitably at his sudden exit, his gown billowing as he made directly for the art room. He hesitated in the doorway long enough to shake his head at the boisterous group inside and to hear Sykes say, 'That's right, lads, we'll get this thing airborne, if it's the last thing we do – and to blazes with the timetable, eh?'

'A word with you, Sykes,' he said coldly, and stepped outside again.

Sykes stood up hesitantly and followed him from the room, turning to say, 'I'll be back in a minute, boys, but see what you can get done without me.'

'What the hell do you think you're doing?' Fordham demanded, as soon as Sykes was with him. 'Who gave you permission to tamper with the timetable?'

'I didn't think a few minutes would matter,' Sykes protested. 'I thought it was more important that the boys finished what they'd started.'

'You thought, did you?' Fordham sneered.

'That's right – and don't take that tone with me. I'm teaching them, remember?'

'What you could teach them, Sykes, I imagine they could learn from the back of a matchbox!' Fordham flinched as Sykes raised a threatening fist, but continued none the less, 'And furthermore, I'll take whatever tone I choose to in the interests of the school.'

'The interests of the school don't come into it,' Sykes

said, poking a finger from his fist almost into Fordham's face. 'You've got it in for me because of Pauline. You're jealous!'

'Don't be absurd,' Fordham hissed, and slapped Sykes' hand aside. 'You're an incompetent, irresponsible lout.'

Sykes swung his fist, but missed as Fordham ducked.

'You're sick with jealousy, I can see it.'

'This has bugger all to do with Pauline, you idiot.'

'You're a bloody liar, Fordham.'

'Call me that again and – '

'Bloody liar!'

Fordham aimed a clumsy punch, which Sykes side-stepped, shoving him away with a straight arm as he came at him again. They faced each other, slightly crouched and panting.

'I think this had better stop,' said Fordham.

Sykes hesitated, then stuck out his hand, which Fordham took.

'Sorry, sir.'

'So am I,' Fordham muttered. 'Damned stupid show.'

Heritage rocked up and down on his plimsolled toes and sketched restless circles with his arms, as he gazed glumly at the rain-streaked window.

'Ah, well,' he sighed. 'I'd've been pushed to make up two teams from the walking wounded. How are your lot doing?' he asked Fordham over his shoulder.

'It's like ten green bottles,' Fordham said from behind a newspaper, 'and the last verse is getting rapidly closer. Siggy back from Lady Arabella's bedside yet?'

Heritage snorted.

'Damned females are causing absolute chaos here this term.'

Fordham put down his paper and said sharply, 'What makes you say that?'

'First George, and now Siggy,' he grunted. 'At least it won't be me next.'

'I think that's a little unfair, Patrick,' Fordham observed, his urbane tone restored. 'Besides we should keep a sense of proportion. In our own chaos we see but a reflection of greater chaos in the world outside.' He waved the paper like a flag. 'Cyprus, Suez, H-bomb tests, terrorism – and at Drummonds Preparatory School, severe outbreaks of love and measles.'

'Mary?'

'Yes?'

'We still haven't really talked about the future, have we?' George murmured. He slipped his hand around her waist and felt the heat from the fire on her blouse. They were stretched out on the hearthrug, his body curved against her back, their walking clothes discarded on the floor behind them.

Mary put her hand on his. 'I don't want to talk about the future,' she said, her voice small and sad. 'I just want to be us, here, now.'

'I know.' George squeezed her gently. 'But that's our problem, darling,' he whispered urgently. 'Tomorrow I have to go back – and what then? These last few hours I've felt you slipping away from me again.'

'I know. I'm sorry, George.'

'But why?' George groaned.

Mary felt for him behind her head and pulled his face against her neck. She stroked the soft bristles on his nape, as she said softly, 'When you asked me to marry you, I so wanted to be the person you needed. I longed to commit myself to you, to the school, to something bigger than myself. I felt a sort of compulsion, almost, to throw myself in at the deep end. But George, it's so very hard to touch bottom in yourself.' She gave his head the lightest tug, and went on, 'You did it years ago, when you found Drummonds, but I'm still floundering.'

'No, darling, no.' George covered her neck with kisses, and his voice was cracked when he spoke again. 'I know I've done badly, but I haven't tried properly. I didn't see, didn't think – '

'I'm not sure I want you to try.' She shook her head, forcing his face away. 'I don't think that's the point at all.'

'But Mary, darling – are you listening?' Mary nodded, and he said, 'If what you want is commitment and stability, I have those in plenty. I thought the problem was something quite different. I thought you found school life dull and rather ridiculous. I even thought you minded seeing so little of me.' He turned her face towards his. 'Mary?'

'Yes,' she said, her eyes filling with tears. 'I minded.'

She pushed herself to her knees, looked away from him, and stood up. For a moment she seemed uncertain what to do, then she went to the record player, twisted a knob on the fascia, lifted the lid and flicked a lever beside the turntable. She watched the arm swing across to the record and sink into the outer groove, before she closed the lid. As the valves warmed, music began to drift from the speaker and the sweet rasp of a tenor saxophone hovered like cigarette smoke in the room. She listened, swaying almost imperceptibly, and then turned slowly to look at George.

'And I'm rotten at sitting on committees and making

small talk with governors' wives,' she said, as if the minutes since she last spoke had not existed, 'but it's more than all that. You see, I felt as if I was disappearing – not waving, but drowning.' She watched George rise and come towards her, as she told him, 'I need to make my own way, find my own stability at last. And, well, I've been offered something – Phillip wants me to go into his antique business with him. He's expanding and –'

George crushed her against him, silencing her voice.

'Darling, I've changed my mind,' he said. 'I don't want to talk any more. Not yet. I just want to hold you and dance with you.'

And they slid into the record's soothing rhythm, their bodies locked tightly together.

11

The bluish pall which hung above the card table in the common room was so dense that, seen on a cinema screen, it would have led mistrustful members of the audience to suspect the presence beside the set in the studio of a team of technicians with smoke guns.

Charles groaned as Heritage declared, 'Four no trumps.'

'Stop signalling,' Fordham told him.

'I wasn't signalling.'

'I distinctly heard you groan.'

Charles frowned at the fan of cards in his hand and said, 'Why do I always have to partner Patrick?'

'Because the good doctor and I are a team, and no one else plays,' Fordham replied, adding somewhat smugly, 'Pass.' His eyes narrowed as he peered beyond the perimeter of smoke, and he said, adopting a tone of theatrical warning, 'Beware ladies.' Then, louder: 'I trust you have been invited, Susan?'

'No,' said Susan, approaching the table.

'Bad form,' Fordham commented, 'uninvited females in the mess.'

'Christopher exaggerates, as ever,' Heritage said, 'but nevertheless . . .'

'Siggy?' Susan asked.

'May I invite you to join us, Susan?'

'Thank you, Siggy.' Susan bowed minutely. 'I accept.'

'Five clubs,' said Charles, and Heritage let out a moan.

'Is that a request for aces?' Fordham demanded.

'What a shower!' Susan observed. 'The only cheerful thing I've seen all day is a letter from Tim Binny, and he's in the madhouse. I want to talk to you – all of you. I want you to put away your cards and listen to me.'

'Your bid, partner,' Fordham said drily.

'Don't be rude, Christopher,' said Charles, and folded his hand. 'If Susan has something to say, we should listen to her.' He reached across the table, took Heritage's cards, and shuffled them together with his own, before dropping the lot in the centre of the table.

'Very neat,' Fordham muttered. 'You've just avoided four down doubled.' He threw his own cards on top of Charles' untidy pile, pushed back his seat and dumped himself in the depths of an armchair, where he hid his face behind a magazine.

'What does Binny have to say?' Gunz asked Susan.

'He seems much happier,' she said, pulling a letter from her pocket and unfolding it. 'This bit's good,' she continued, and began to read aloud: '"Did you know that this place is run by the LCC, of which it is a faithful mirror, that is CCL, which stands for Cloud Cuckoo Land." And he says his Bible classes are well attended,' she added.

'At last!' Gunz exclaimed.

'But at least all that God business gave him a sense of purpose,' Susan went on. 'Where's ours? What's the matter with us all? Sir goes round looking like something excavated from a tomb –'

She checked herself, and said, 'I'm sorry, Charles, but it's absolutely true,' punctuating her apology with a shrug. 'The maids are moping – well, Pauline certainly is. And as for you lot – '

'Us lot?' Charles prodded her.

'February in person,' Susan sighed, 'and I can't stand it. So I'm going to organize something – a breath of fresh air.'

'I hope you're not going to open the windows,' Heritage growled. 'It's freezing outside.'

'I'm going to invite someone to the school.'

'Damn good idea,' said Fordham.

'I'm sorry?' Susan said, as if she was hard of hearing.

'To invite someone down,' explained Fordham. 'And I've found the very person.' He indicated a photograph in the magazine and, seeing Charles' inquiring look, tossed it to him.

'Yes, indeed,' Charles agreed, and announced, 'Marilyn Monroe.'

'She'd definitely liven the place up,' said Fordham, beaming broadly. 'And, what's more, it says she's in the country right now, making a film. So you have my whole-hearted support, Susan.'

Gunz frowned at him and said severely, 'I think Susan was being serious.'

'Thank you, Siggy. My suggestion – ' she began, but was interrupted by Braithwaite's bustling arrival.

'Evening one and all.' His greeting boomed across the common room. 'Poor old George, still no letter,' he said with a disconsolate shake of his head, then added hurriedly, 'No offence meant, Charles, merely a genuine expression of sympathy.' He shook his head again. 'Poor George.'

'What on earth are you blathering on about, Bertie?' Fordham demanded.

'George is expecting a letter, that's all, and the lady's not writing.'

'How can you know that?' Susan said in a voice of reproval.

'I'm positive of it,' Braithwaite replied. 'She's dropped George, dropped her job with Leo, and gone off with some fellow in the furniture business.'

'He's an antique dealer and a homosexual,' Charles corrected him. 'And I don't think it's any business of ours anyway.'

Braithwaite reddened at this rebuke, but said, 'Quite right, Charles, well said – no business of ours at all.'

'On the contrary,' said Susan, causing the others to look askance at her. 'Sir's in the dumps and we're in the dumps. It connects – everything connects.'

'Send for Marilyn Monroe, I say.'

'Shut up, Chris,' Susan scolded. 'That's why I'm going to organise a painting competition for the boys. And if George agrees, I'll ask Meredith Ross down to judge it.'

'Friend of yours?' Fordham inquired, teasing her with a smile.

Susan looked at him levelly. 'Yes, he used to be,' she said.

'Kitchen sink school, isn't he?'

'Neo-realism, please, Chris,' Gunz advised him.

'Kitchen sink'll do,' shrugged Susan. 'There's quite a lot of domestic porcelain in Meredith's work.'

'Meredith Ross?' Braithwaite murmured, frowning. 'I'm sure I've seen his name somewhere recently. He was kicked out of some do or other for not having the right clothes on – that the chap?'

Susan showed a slight smile, and said, 'Sounds as if it could be.'

'Well, I don't want to be a wet blanket, but I don't think you'll get a lot of joy out of George.'

'Why ever not?'

'If you knew how long it's taken me to get him to even consider some of my plans, Susan, you'd understand – and very modest proposals at that, believe me. Let's face it, inviting a chap like that down is a pretty unconventional notion, isn't it.'

'Is it?'

'So I suggest you don't stress the, well, radical side of things. If you could somehow present the idea in a traditional way, though I don't quite know how –'

'Yes, I see,' Susan broke in a trifle hurriedly. 'That's very useful. Thanks.'

Braithwaite rubbed his chin.

'I've always found in my dealings with George, that avoiding the radical approach yields the best results.'

'Mmmm, yes, thanks,' Susan mumbled, nodding her head vigorously in a show of earnest appreciation.

'I'd still prefer Marilyn Monroe,' Fordham muttered.

Susan turned her thumb up triumphantly at Charles, as they almost collided in the outer door of Dorothy's office, and said delightedly, 'Like a lamb.'

Charles gave her shoulder a pat of congratulation.

'The Braithwaite method?' he inquired, and Susan gave a little giggle as she continued into the corridor, while he eyed Dorothy with a nod in the direction of the inner door and Dorothy motioned him towards it.

'Come!' George called in answer to Charles' knock, but sat up stiffly when he entered, as if he had been disturbed unexpectedly.

'Have you got a moment?' Charles asked hesitantly.

'Of course.'

'I feel a bit awkward about this,' Charles began uneasily, 'but I wondered if there was any news from Mary.' He watched his father's head jerk back with indignation, and continued quickly. 'There's a lot of ridiculous gossip flying around, which I feel quite powerless to stop. And not just in the common room and the kitchen – Christopher confiscated a rather scurrilous vignette, although he took no action against its grubby little author.'

'Gossip about Mary?' George asked sternly, and grimaced when Charles said, 'Yes.'

'I suppose it was inevitable,' Charles observed, 'but I don't like listening to it. And there's nothing I can do about it, because I'm as much in the dark as the rest of them. But I wanted to tell you that I'm on your side – and Mary's too. So if there's anything I could say that would shut them up.' He hesitated. 'If you wanted to tell me, of course.'

'Dear Charles,' said George, smiling weakly, 'thank you for being on Mary's side as well as mine – and yes, she has written.' He spread his fingers across a handwritten sheet of notepaper which lay in front of him on his desk, and sighed. 'She thinks we should remain apart for the time being. Not see each other.'

'I'm sorry.'

'She has some idea that we should try to rediscover ourselves, as she puts it, as individuals.'

'So it isn't finished?'

'She says not.'

'Good. What do you say?'

George's hand began to slap the desk. 'I don't know,' he said, but then: 'I think it is – I think it's finished.'

'Why?' Charles urged him.

'Because what she's implying is impossible,' George replied hopelessly.

'And what is she implying?'

'That we should continue openly, as it were,' said George, his voice unsteady with embarrassment. 'How could I?' he demanded. 'Dear God, she's a parent, apart from anything else. It could destroy the school.'

'Drummonds, *c'est moi,*' Charles intoned solemnly.

'Oh, for God's sake, Charles!' George snapped.

'I'm sorry, father, I didn't mean that. But why shouldn't it be open? It's not as if either of you are married to anyone else.'

'Nor are we married to each other – and that's why not. Like it or not, those are the rules of the society we live in. I'm preparing boys to take their place in that society.'

'You may take your place in society provided you make life a misery for yourself, is that it?'

'Provided you do your duty!'

Charles shoved a hand through his hair. 'That's out of the ark, father. No one believes that any more.'

'I do,' George said evenly. 'By the way, how's Wendy?'

'What?'

'She's been looking after you for almost a fortnight. I thought you might know – or even perhaps care.'

'That's not fair, Dad,' Charles protested.

'Out of the ark as well, eh?'

Charles rolled his eyes to the ceiling and took a deep breath before murmuring, 'She's fine, absolutely fine.'

There was a silence and then George said, 'I think I should go and see her.'

'Mary?'

'I want to sort this thing out face to face.'

'But that's precisely what she doesn't want you to do.'

'So she says.'

'It sounds to me as if she means it.'

George had been toying distractedly with a corner of Mary's letter as he talked, but now he leaned across his desk and looked hard at his son, and told him, 'I think I know her a little better than you do.'

'Oh, that's great,' muttered Charles, and shook his head as if confounded by an unfathomable enigma. Then he turned towards the door, pausing before he opened it to say fiercely, 'I'll tell you something, though. You want to see her because you're scared to death. Scared of being anything that isn't a headmaster – of being yourself, of being alone, of being one of those individuals this school is so proud of turning out.'

George slowly reread Mary's letter, hearing her voice and wondering how well he really did know her or indeed, during these unsettling recent weeks, how well he knew himself.

A thunderous glissando beyond the school boundary took the attention of every boy and adult in the reception party even before the motorbike materialized between the school gates. As it roared up the drive towards them, the shape in the saddle separated into the distinct outlines of rider and pillion passenger, dressed in leather jacket and goggles, and when the first shut off the motor and shoved his goggles up on to his forehead, Susan said, somewhat shyly, 'Hello, Meredith.'

'Hello, love,' the rider replied cheerfully. He tugged the silent machine up on to its stand, cocked a leg across the petrol tank and grinned at her. His passenger dismounted first, unhitching the skirt of an evening gown which had been tucked up out of the way of the wheel spokes, and releasing a cascade of blonde hair from the confines of the jacket collar, both operations so enthralling the assembled audience that most missed the bear-hug of an embrace to which Ross treated

Susan, before holding her appraisingly at arms' length and telling her, 'You'll do, in fact, you'll more than do. What a gift!' Susan smiled at this, as Ross continued, 'And just to show you how much I love you, here's my latest lady. Suzy, meet Suzy.'

'You see,' he explained, as they shook hands, 'they all have to be called Susan.' Then he turned to George and said, 'Mr Drummond?'

'Yes.'

'Ross.'

And he shook George's hand heartily.

'Welcome to Drummonds, Mr Ross.'

'Thanks,' said Ross. 'Glad to be here. Excuse the togs – we've come from a party.' He unzipped his jacket to show his evening clothes, then slapped the saddle of his motorbike. 'What do you think of the machine? Isn't she beautiful?'

'Magnificent,' Gunz agreed, his eyes gleaming.

'I bought it from a chap at the party.'

As the boys moved in to admire it, he said a loud hullo, and in response to the scattered greetings they returned, cupped his hand behind his ear and bellowed like a pantomime performer at a matinée, 'What was that?'

'Hello, sir!' the boys chorused back.

'Much better!' He clapped his hands, and said, 'Sir, eh? I like that. Sir for an afternoon. Excellent! Now, Susan, where are these paintings? I like to take my time looking at pictures.'

As Susan led the way to the art room, Ross linked one arm through hers and the other through his blonde companion's, and not even a pipe and piebald outfit could have had the crowd tagging more compliantly behind him. He asked to be left alone to judge the competition, and when Susan detached herself from the excited throng in the corridor outside to inquire about his progress, he stood back and said, 'Some of this is marvellous, really good. And I've got my winner,' he added, indicating a still life. 'All his own work?'

'Yes.'

'He can put it on paper, that one.'

'I know.'

'So this is your life, Suzy,' he said, looking round the room. 'Is it good? It looks it. We never painted like this at school. And how are you? You look all right.'

'What did you mean, "what a gift"?'

Ross grinned. 'Your looking so terrific was like getting a present for me.'

'I can't tell you what a relief it is to see you.'

'Didn't you think I'd turn up?' he asked, in an injured tone.

'No, not that.'

'Oh.'

'I was right about you,' she said, 'but I was fantasizing – just a little.'

'No more fantasies?'

'No.' She looked away, then back to his eyes. 'What about the other Suzy?'

'Just indulging my eternal immaturity – like now,' he added, and pulled her into a kiss.

When they separated, Susan said, 'That was just for old times' sake.'

'For old times' sake,' Ross echoed softly.

'A necessary exorcism.'

They stood smiling at one another until Ross tilted his head towards the gallery of pictures.

'You know there's only one painter among the lot of them,' he said, 'one *real* painter.'

'I'm afraid you've got to choose two others.'

Ross scanned the boys' work again, and winked at

Susan. 'I'll have them for you by the time you get that lot out there in here,' he assured her.

When everyone had streamed in and settled in front of him, Ross waved a hand at the paintings and declared, 'I'm impressed. This is good stuff. But I've been told to pick a winner, and I have done. Anybody think they're the winner?' he asked.

The painter of the still life was standing close to Susan, and she caught his eye as meaningfully as she could as his hand appeared from his pocket, then dropped out of sight again.

'Well, there is someone in this room who's a real painter,' Ross went on, 'and he knows who he is, and he knows he should be the winner, and he knows he doesn't need me to tell him, although I'm going to give him a big hint.' He beamed at the confused faces below him. 'Is this all a bit mysterious for you? Well, it's meant to be. Now,' he announced, 'I want every boy who submitted a painting to the competition to step forward.' He waited while the entrants pushed their way to the front, before continuing, 'I had a piece of luck yesterday, boys. I sold a painting. I didn't want to sell it, so I named an outrageous price, and I got it. Such is life. Now I happen to believe luck should be shared, so . . .'

Instead of finishing what he was saying, he dipped his hand into his pocket and pulled out a wad of pound notes, from which he peeled one after another until all the astonished entrants had been rewarded.

'There we are,' he said, stuffing the still plump remainder of his money back in his pocket. 'Don't spend it all on fast cars and women. And now I'm going to ask your lovely art mistress for some paper which we can use as ballot slips, so you can each vote for your favourite painting – but you're not allowed to choose your own, mind,' he warned, as he helped Susan tear up and distribute the scraps of paper.

'You certainly have the touch, Mr Ross,' George remarked admiringly, while the boys milled around the table where Susan had stationed herself as teller.

'Fun, isn't it?'

'Do you think they'll choose your painter?'

'They'd have to be insanely mature,' Ross replied with a frown. 'I wouldn't wish that on them.'

When at last Susan handed him a fold of paper and the buzz of excited chatter dipped to an expectant hum, Ross glanced at the note, grinned and said, 'Well, it was very close, but we now know who you chose, and voters, I want you to make a vow – a vow to keep a secret. And the secret is which painting you chose. Agreed?'

'Agreed!'

'Now I'm going to tell you something,' Ross continued. 'People are successful in this life for three reasons – because they believe in themselves, because other people believe in them, or because they take risks. I'm going to buy three of your paintings, and when I'm gone, you're going to wonder which is the painting painted by our real winner, which is the risky painting, and which is the one you all chose, and you're going to have to make your own minds up, because the mystery will never be resolved for you. Don't forget, you've vowed not to tell which one you voted for. And you painters whose paintings I didn't buy must decide if you believe in yourselves or if other people believe in you or if you are one of those people who are condemned in this life to the marvellous fun of risk taking.' He paused momentarily, then announced the titles of the winning paintings.

George called at once for three cheers, and his hearty

'Hip hip' was answered each time by a resounding roar.

'Thank you, Susan,' he said later, as they watched Ross's bike accelerate away into the evening, 'I do believe your breath of fresh air has done the trick.' He turned to Charles and murmured, 'Who would've believed it?' Then he took his son's arm and said, 'I owe you an apology, Charles. I haven't been behaving terribly well of late, have I?'

'You've been all right.'

'No, I haven't.'

'Understandable, though.'

'Well, I'm not going to let her go,' George said determinedly. 'I'm going to ring her tonight. Start talking again.'

'Attaboy,' said Charles, and clapped his father on the back.

12

Susan unlocked the art-room cupboard and disappeared inside, re-emerging with a bottle of scotch and two tumblers. She peered into these, grimaced, and went to the nearest sink, where she rinsed one under the cold tap, and since the towel rail beneath the sink was empty, she flicked away as much water as she could with a jerk of her wrist.

When she saw Gunz examining the medieval sun she had drawn on the blackboard, she said, 'When I saw all the boys' work displayed in the competition, it all looked so haphazard somehow, so I decided I should have a theme for the rest of the term, and that's it – the sun.'

'Potent symbol,' Gunz observed.

'Actually I didn't have much choice,' Susan continued, as she filled the glasses. 'The stupid suppliers mucked up the order and delivered double orange and yellow and no blues or greens.'

Siggy laughed and she handed him a glass, before raising her own.

'Thanks, Siggy.'

'What on earth for?' Gunz asked, raising his in turn.

'For coming with me to see Tim. I know you weren't very fond of him.'

'It was a pleasure,' Gunz insisted. 'It always is being with you.'

'He seems fine, doesn't he?'

'Certainly,' Gunz said, nodding agreement. 'If anything, he seems far too happy in that wretched place.'

'Yes,' said Susan, and took a contemplative sip. 'And are we too?'

'In our wretched place?' Gunz poked his chin out doubtfully. 'Perhaps.'

Susan raised her glass again, vaguely. 'Anyway, thanks for sparing the time.'

'From what?'

'From your other life, of course,' she said, smiling.

'Aah,' Gunz sighed, 'yes, my *other* life – that's most accurate.'

'Will you go on teaching?'

Gunz laughed unhappily. 'How observant, Susan,' he said, sighing again. 'Yes, teaching was a bit of an issue in my other life.'

'Was?' Susan asked hesitantly.

'I no longer have another life.'

'Oh, Siggy.'

'I've written Arabella a letter.' He took a drink and added disconsolately, 'The coward's way.'

'But you've left her?'

'I think I have, yes.'

'Don't you know?'

'I can't believe it at the moment,' Gunz said, and shook his head, 'but, yes, I think I have.'

'You don't sound totally heartbroken,' Susan said, when she caught his eye.

'Don't I?' he inquired. 'No, what I feel most is relief. I feel as if I've escaped a terrible humiliation.'

'Whatever do you mean?'

'I think I was about to be packed off to join Arabella's old rocking horse and her doll's house.'

'Well done, Siggy! It's brave of you to put yourself in that category,' Susan laughed. 'I must say I've never seen you as a rich woman's toy.'

'You can laugh, Susan,' Gunz protested, 'but it's very disturbing, I can tell you, to wake up one morning and say to yourself, 'Look here, you are an ageing, balding, intellectual gigolo – what are you doing here?' He shook his head emphatically, and went on, 'At any moment I was going to be asked to go hunting – and I hate horses. They're bigger than me and they never do what I tell them.'

'Have another drink,' Susan suggested, after Gunz had drained his glass with a shudder.

'Thank you,' Gunz said, and held out the glass while she refilled it. 'I dreaded the questions most, I think. They're always asking questions, you know, trying to place you, to categorize you. "Do you like books? Do you like Oxford Street? Conversation? Do you disapprove of bloodsports? Tell me, old man, do Jews hunt?" As if there is a pig at the bottom of it somewhere. Well, I'll tell you what!'

'What?' asked Susan, looking alarmed by Gunz's growing agitation.

'This morning at breakfast I said to the butler, "Look here, Ridgeon, I want some gefilte fish instead of those kippers." You should've seen his face – it was a picture. I tell you, I'll remember it longer than the Gainsboroughs and the Constables.'

Susan laughed uneasily. 'What is this all of a sudden?' she asked. 'I never knew that was an issue with you.'

'It wasn't, until George started making an issue of it,' Gunz said flatly. 'But the effect has been to sensitize me.'

'George?' Susan asked, surprised. 'Why George?'

'He thinks we have an outbreak of anti-Semitism in the school. Do you know Steiner?'

'A rather miserable-looking creature in the middle school?'

Gunz nodded. 'That's the one.'

'What evidence does he have?'

'There is evidence of bullying – I've witnessed it myself more than once, including an unsavoury incident when his shorts and socks were removed and his bare feet were blacked with boot polish.' He opened his hands in a gesture of uncertainty, and added, 'But just because English schoolboys can behave like barbarians doesn't mean they are anti-Jewish.'

'So what makes George think they are?' Susan asked. 'Just because Steiner's Jewish?'

'Barton was heard to call him a yid.'

'Is he the ringleader?'

'Yes.'

'A nasty piece of work, that one.'

'But an anti-Semite? At the age of eleven?'

Susan frowned. 'Has anyone spoken to the boy?'

'Steiner?' Siggy asked, and Susan nodded. 'Yes, I have myself. He seems to have no sense of Jewishness, let alone being picked on because of it,' he explained with a shrug. 'I don't know whether George is right or not, but I look at the poor unattractive little blighter and, frankly, whether he's a victim of circumstance or something more sinister hardly seems to matter.'

'Come in, Siggy,' George said, and waved him at once to a chair. 'I thought you ought to know, there's been another nasty development.' He waited until Gunz was seated, and went on, 'I happened to see Steiner drop something into one of the dustbins. It was his cap. Some nauseating animal had urinated in it.'

'Barton again?' Gunz growled, his face screwed up with disgust.

'If I was sure, I would've thrashed him,' George barked, then said more steadily, 'I'm afraid we have to face the fact that there's some very unpleasant bullying going on.'

'And you're still convinced that it's anti-Semitism?'

'More so than ever. Once these things take hold, they're very hard to root out. I want it stopped now.'

'Of course.'

There was a pause, then George added, 'And I was rather counting on your help.'

Gunz shifted slightly in his seat, and said, 'You have it, George. Only I'm not convinced you're right.'

'I see.'

'I can't think I wouldn't have noticed something,' Gunz continued. 'I know how these things start.'

'I know you do,' George broke in. 'That's why – '

Gunz stopped him with a hand. 'I understand that, and it's very decent of you. No more than I would expect – that's what I felt when I first came to Drummonds. I tell you, George, it seemed like paradise. A decent corner of a decent country. And believe me, I'd seen enough ugliness in Vienna to last me a lifetime.'

'Siggy, I'm sorry to insist,' George said awkwardly, 'but there's something very ugly going on here.'

'But I've spoken to the boy,' Gunz insisted.

'I think the problem is that you don't want to believe it could happen here, and it's very gratifying that you feel that way – to all of us. But I fear you're idealizing us, Siggy. You don't want a note of discord to ruin your idea of Drummonds.'

Gunz contradicted him with a shake of his head. 'I believe in evidence, George,' he explained. 'What you're suggesting – a little clique of dyed-in-the-wool Jew baiters – that's not the kind of something which is in the atmosphere, which happens to materialize one day. It starts with an individual, a pernicious individual, and remember, we're talking about children. I haven't seen such a child.'

'Damn it, Siggy, Steiner's being bullied. There's no getting away from it. He's been physically attacked and he's been humiliated . . .'

'May I say something?' Siggy interrupted.

'Go ahead,' George said warily.

'I think you're being over-sensitive about this business of Jewishness,' he said, and a gentle laugh bubbled from his throat. 'I am myself over-polite to the Indian gentlemen who issue me with my ticket on London buses. It is a gentle fault, but it is none the less a fault. By being so sensitive, you see, you show us that you're uncomfortable about us.' He paused while George offered a begrudging grunt of comprehension, then said, 'I shall get to the bottom of this business for you, George. I'll need to take tomorrow afternoon off.'

George frowned. 'It's half term soon.'

'Half term won't do.'

'Very well.'

Gunz stood up, but checked himself as he turned towards the door. 'Look, George,' he said, 'I know you think I haven't been as co-operative as I might have been. But I hope you also know how much I appreciate your concern.' He turned away again, and was gone before George could shape an answering word or a gesture.

*

Because he was unacquainted with the suburbs of south London, Gunz stopped to consult his dog-eared A1 guide at each street corner, once he had ascertained which route to take from the underground station; but eventually, and not a little apprehensively, he found himself beside the front gate of a detached house with net curtains at every window in spite of the fact that the windows were separated from the pavement by a neat expanse of garden and the interior which the curtains hid appeared gloomy enough to prohibit prying eyes. He compared the number on the gate with the one he had written next to the name of the street in his notebook, pushed the gate open and walked up to the front door, searching the windows anxiously for signs of habitation. After a perfunctory press on the bell push, he stepped back and surveyed the windows again, then leaned on it longer, until a curtain twitched behind the opaque glass panel that filled the door at eye level and he heard a woman's voice say something unintelligible.

'Sorry?' he called, his mouth close to the letter box.

'Who is it?' came the nervous question.

'My name is Dr Gunz. I am a master from the school – from Drummonds.'

'Wait a moment.'

Behind the door several bolts were drawn, and it opened six inches, a chain stretched taut across the gap, where a woman's face appeared.

'Mrs Steiner?'

The face bobbed in the dim light of the hallway.

'Sorry to trouble you, Mrs Steiner. Don't worry, I haven't come with news of a disaster. But if I might come in?'

The door banged shut, and stayed closed long enough

for Gunz to mop the perspiration generated by a brisk walk from his brow with a handkerchief, before it opened again, this time wide enough to allow him inside.

'You'd better come through into the lounge,' Mrs Steiner said, opening a door to the right of the hall without noticeably lightening the gloom. Then she told him in a warning voice, 'This is the day my husband comes home early. I don't think you'd better be here then.'

'Ah,' said Gunz, 'I was hoping to see you both.'

'No, I don't think so.'

'I was very much hoping so.'

'Oh dear,' fussed Mrs Steiner, 'were you? I don't know if Mr Steiner will like that. The groceries came today,' she added, as if in explanation.

'I see,' Gunz said helpfully, and sat down.

'I'd better make a cup of tea.'

The longer Mrs Steiner was gone, the more uncomfortable and untidy Gunz felt amongst the clinically clean furnishings of her sitting room, and when she appeared in the doorway he got up to take the single cup she carried. But she stopped and said, 'Would you like a biscuit?'

'I'm all right, thanks,' Gunz replied, and watched helplessly as she went again.

When she returned a second time, one hand held the cup and saucer and the other a plate with a single biscuit at its centre, but no sooner had Gunz accepted them with effusive thanks prompted by a look which implored him for approval, than she was out of the room once more, drawn by the rattle of the front door. As he sipped unwillingly at the warm, weak tea, Gunz listened to a murmur of conversation punctuated by angry interjections from a voice that clearly belonged to Mr Steiner, but the man was smiling, if somewhat tensely, when he entered the sitting room.

'Good of you to come, Mr . . .'

'Gunz – Dr Gunz.' He made an effort to rise, but with nowhere to put his cup and afraid of dislodging the plate from the arm of the chair, sat down again to Mrs Steiner's undisguised relief.

'Mr Goons,' repeated Mr Steiner, pronouncing the name like the radio series that was so popular with some boys at school. 'Michael Steiner. You've come to see us about young Harry, have you?'

'That's right, Mr Steiner, I have.'

'He hasn't been a bad boy, has he?'

'No, no,' Gunz assured him quickly. 'He doesn't get into trouble.'

'His reports are always most satisfactory,' said Mrs Steiner, but bit her lip when her husband rounded on her.

'I dare say, my dear, that Mr Goons here,' he said sourly, persevering with his mispronunciation, 'is probably well aware of that.' He discouraged further participation in the conversation with a harsh look, and turned his back on her. 'So what's it all about, Mr Goons?' he inquired in a voice that could have come from someone else. But when Gunz hesitated, he demanded, 'He's not ill, is he?'

'No, no, it's nothing like that. It's just that – well, let's say your boy doesn't hold his own very well, Mr Steiner.'

'Are you saying the boy is being bullied?'

'I'm afraid it's not quite as simple as that.'

'I won't have him bullied, Mr Goons.'

'He lets himself down,' Gunz explained carefully. 'He lets himself in for it, you know.'

'That's what they always say, isn't it?' Mr Steiner

sneered. 'He's a Jew, he brings it on himself,' he mimicked. 'I thought it was supposed to be a nice school.'

'I think it is.'

'Naturally you would. But they still call a spade a spade, eh? And a yid a yid?'

'I think perhaps I ought to make it clear that I'm Jewish myself, and I really did think at first that some – not all – of your son's problems might be due to some form of racial bullying, but – '

'But what?'

'And I resisted the idea that he was some sort of natural victim,' Gunz continued, ignoring the interruption. 'I've heard that argument too often. I think in your son's case, there is a form of profound unhappiness.'

'What's he been saying?'

'Nothing, I can assure you. This is all intuition and guesswork.' Gunz shrugged, and told him, 'I think your son is unhappy, and I felt I should bring this to your attention.'

'Very good of you, I'm sure.' Mr Steiner looked suddenly and deeply suspicious. 'But what are you saying, Mr Goons?'

'Saying, Mr Steiner?'

'You say the boy's unhappy. So what does this mean? What's the big event? You're saying something else, aren't you?'

'No, I'm not, I can assure you. Happiness is . . .' Gunz paused, and his hands searched the air for words. 'People need happiness – I mean biologically need it. I really believe that. To me unhappiness is an important event. In the surroundings of a little English school perhaps it's tempting to think of such things as trivial, but that is not my feeling. No, I think the boy is turned against himself – and no good can come of it.'

'So what are you saying?' Mr Steiner demanded again. 'You're telling me I should have the boy home? What are you saying?'

'I don't know,' Gunz replied gravely. 'I was hoping you might be able to tell me. I felt it was important to discuss.'

'Perhaps –' Mrs Steiner began, but her husband snapped, 'Be quiet. So maybe the boy wasn't so happy at home. Maybe he's just not a very happy little boy. Maybe it's not in his nature.'

'I'm a scientist, Mr Steiner. It's in my nature to think that an effect has a cause.'

'You're saying we make our Harry unhappy?' Mr Steiner asked, his voice rising with anger. 'That's nice. I don't need to be told that, Mr Goons, I don't need that. I pay you to get him into a public school, that's what I pay you for – not to give me a lecture about the way I treat him. Harry's said something?'

'Nothing. Please, Mr Steiner, I didn't say that. I'm sure you treat him impeccably.'

'I treat him like a prince,' Mr Steiner hissed defiantly, 'that's how I treat him. Nothing's too good for that boy. From birth, the red carpet.'

'You should have seen his pram,' said Mrs Steiner, unable to stop herself.

'Be quiet!' Mr Steiner rounded on her again. 'Do you think the man wants to know about his pram?' But turning to Gunz, he said, 'I tell you, that pram was coach-built. Fit for royalty. That's how he's always been treated – like royalty!'

'I'm sure he has,' Gunz agreed, anxious to escape the interview.

'You see!' said Mrs Steiner.

'How would he know? Eh?' Mr Steiner demanded.

'How would you know, Mr Goons? The circus came to town, the boy was there – in the front row. Theatre. Music. Some people give their children things. What are things? Mere money! I gave my boy experiences. The best. Paris? He's been there. The British Museum? Sutton Hoo? You name it, he's seen it.'

'The mummies gave him bad dreams,' Mrs Steiner pointed out.

'Of course they did! You show a boy a dead body, what does he do? Of course he has bad dreams. What are you saying? We don't give him experiences because of Boris Karloff? What do you want? To stunt the boy? Should he have Enid Blyton and hot-water bottles? Be serious.' Then his wife was excluded once again, as Mr Steiner said to Gunz, 'You see what I'm saying? I've done my bit for the boy, Mr Goons, now I expect you to do yours.'

Gunz was only too eager to agree. He skimped the formalities of farewell to the perimeter of politeness, hurried along the paved front path without even a glance over his shoulder at the sepulchral façade, and stopped only when he had turned a corner that took him out of sight of the Steiners' street. Then he leaned against a pillar box, loosened his tie, and gulped in air as if he had emerged from a fetid cavern. He found he was sweating, and that his sweat stank. He moved on slowly towards the underground station.

George was waiting for him and called his name, interrupting Gunz's satisfying calculation of the number of footsteps that would take him to an armchair in the common room. He turned wearily in the direction of the headmaster's voice and asked without interest, 'What is it?'

'I think you should come with me,' George said severely. 'There's something you should see.'

Gunz followed him to the art room, finding the pace disagreeably fast at the end of a long and trying afternoon. He asked him once on the way what the matter was, but received no answer until George threw open the door and said, 'That!' Squeezing past him, he followed George's pointing finger to the blackboard, where a swastika, a yard across, was emblazoned. His mouth went slack with astonishment, but then the corners started slowly to stretch and lift into an enormous grin, and Gunz began to giggle.

As George turned, with a look as horrified as his had been, Gunz stifled his giggling sufficiently to say, 'My dear fellow, it's part of Susan's subject, you know, her theme for the term.'

'A swastika?' George asked, still incredulous.

'Yes, it represents the sun. That's why the Nazis' appropriation of it is such an evil perversion.'

'The sun,' George muttered.

'Yes, it's an ancient symbol – an Aryan fire sign.' Gunz squeezed his arm lightly, and added, 'This business is getting the better of us, George.'

'I think you're right,' George sighed. 'Why don't you come and tell me how your afternoon went?' he suggested, but seeing the tiredness in Gunz's face and sagging frame, said, 'Or perhaps tomorrow morning will do just as well.'

George dropped the receiver abruptly on to its rest when a man's voice answered Mary's telephone instead of hers, a voice, as far as he could ascertain from half a dozen words, which did not belong to Phillip Bennett either. While he was regretting his hasty reaction, more suited to a smarting adolescent than a middle-aged man and which now made a second call impossibly embarrassing, his discomfort was alleviated by a knock on his study door. His answering invitation admitted Wendy.

'Yes?' George asked her.

'I thought I ought to let you know that Rodney Middle are having a dorm feast,' she explained. 'Barton got a cake.'

'Thank you for telling me, Wendy. We have to allow them the occasional clandestine thrill, I suppose, but if you wouldn't mind checking that it's over by eleven-thirty or so, I'd be very grateful.'

'Of course,' Wendy said and left.

But the news of late-night celebrations in a dormitory occupied by Barton and Steiner made George uneasy, and long before the curfew he had asked Wendy to impose, he made his way quietly along the corridor towards the door of Rodney Middle dorm. At first all he heard as he approached were excited whispers, then a thump, a crash, and a jumble of furious cries created a cacophonous prelude to Steiner's wild-eyed appearance in the doorway where, hesitating, he was caught in the midriff by a shoulder charge from Barton, the momentum knocking him backwards across the corridor as he fell, so that his head thudded sickeningly against the skirting on the opposite wall. Barton was on him instantly, alternately drumming his chest with both fists and raining punches at his head, all the time screaming, 'Stupid bloody yid! Stupid bloody bastard Jew! Yid! Yid! Yid . . .' With each word another fist landed in Steiner's face, and Barton's fury deafened him to George's thunderous commands until he was dragged from Steiner's bloodied, cowering form. Even then, panting from anger and effort, he said again with venom in his voice: 'Jew!'

George pushed him roughly away. 'Go downstairs and wait outside my study,' he ordered. 'Now! And you others, return to your beds at once – I'll see you all in the morning.' Then, as Wendy arrived at a run, he helped Steiner to his feet and said, 'What happened, Steiner?' But he did not press the boy when he did not answer.

Wendy said, 'Come on, you little horror, I'd better get you cleaned up,' and as she led him gently towards the bathroom with a comforting arm around his shoulders, George noticed that one of Steiner's feet was covered in chocolate.

'He trod in the cake? Deliberately?' Susan's voice rose in amazement.

Gunz nodded unhappily.

'And Barton?'

'Out on his ear.' Gunz shook his head. 'There is a pernicious child,' he muttered. 'George was talking about learning lessons from history, but I'm not sure what we've witnessed has much to do with history. It seems to me it's more a quirk of the human soul, and as such, unfortunately, will always be with us – though not, I hope, again in this school.' Gunz grunted. 'Ironically, Barton may have done Steiner a favour.'

'How?' said Susan.

'If all this hadn't happened, he might have just drifted past us, unnoticed except to be unliked and terminally unhappy. Would any of us have bothered much? I'm not sure I would. But the moment I entered that house, I could smell poison in the air, and Steiner's breathed it since birth, poor little brat. In spite of what went on tonight, I think this school's the only hope for him. If we can raise his expectations of the world just a little.' Gunz had been staring at the floor between his knees, but looked at Susan as he said, 'I think one's treatment by other people is mostly determined by one's expectations of them, don't you?'

'The trouble is, Siggy, that however sympathetic we may feel about the horrendous way he's been victimized by Barton, it doesn't actually make him any more likeable as a human being.'

Susan waved her empty glass in front of Gunz's face, and he started as if the movement of its glinting surface had snapped him out of hypnosis.

'I'm so sorry, Susan,' he said, grabbing a bottle from the floor beside his foot. 'Mine too.' When both glasses were refilled, he returned to her answer. 'I agree, but the boy has to be helped.'

'By you?'

'I can't imagine who else.'

'I don't know, Siggy, I find some of this very suspect.'

Gunz was about to drink, but took the glass abruptly from his mouth. 'What?' he asked her.

'I just wonder about your motives,' she said. 'I wonder how honest you are with yourself.' She hesitated at Gunz's baffled look, but went on, 'Two things. Listen. You want a child to look after – a son – very understandable, most of us do. I suppose you pick on Steiner because effectively he's an orphan. Fine, but there are actual orphans at the school. So why Steiner, Siggy?'

Gunz stared at her, but said nothing.

'I'll tell you why,' Susan continued, 'because you're afraid of happiness. You want someone as difficult as Steiner so you need have no expectations of him. The point about Steiner is that he'll *never* let you down.'

'You're very clever, Susan,' Gunz observed, but she brushed his interruption aside.

'Nothing to do with it. I'm interested, that's all. It's the same with Arabella. She could have given you your freedom. You looked so happy sometimes when you came back from seeing her. I'm interested how you can chuck that away.'

Gunz folded his arms defensively, crooking his glass in his elbow. 'I didn't feel it to be real,' he murmured.

'I think you were so unused to being happy, it scared you to death. "Let's get out now, before we forget what mediocrity feels like!"'

'My God!' he protested. 'If I thought you were right!'

Susan smiled. 'And aren't I?' she asked quietly.

'I don't know!' Gunz sprang up from the side of his narrow bed and paced over to the window. 'Really I don't know,' he insisted. 'I think there may be some truth in what you say about Steiner. I don't know. But I'll tell you something about Lady Arabella. She wants a change of scenery? She takes it – she goes to Gstaad. I prefer a book. True! She goes to Gstaad, I am reading Tinbergen. She is a person whose pleasure is distraction. I am a person whose pleasure is concentration. It's as simple as that.'

'So bloody what!' said Susan, more vehemently than she intended. 'She made you happy, Siggy, for God's sake.'

'And that's another thing,' Gunz said, his eyes shining. 'A conversation like this between Arabella and me could never have taken place. Shall I tell you why?' he demanded.

'Why?'

'Because she wasn't interested enough in me. She wasn't interested enough to begin thinking in the way you have. I'm not totally blind about my own happiness. You are perceptive about my relations with the world, Susan.' He held out his glass in the space between them and closed one eye, so her face was hidden from him. 'I wonder why,' he remarked sadly, 'I wonder why you bother.'

'Why indeed?' Susan said softly, bringing up her own glass to clink against his. 'Well, we've got plenty of time to find out, now that you're back inside. I think you're mad, but here you are.' And she clinked his glass again.

13

The staff meeting ground inexorably on, its agenda a routine repertoire of administrative minutiae whose interminable appearances meant each item was raised, discussed and dismissed without argument or enthusiasm. George's proposal of a staff subscription to provide a present for Pauline on the occasion of her imminent leave aroused momentary controversy when Heritage objected gruffly on the grounds that she had been at the school less than a year and would in any case be returning, or so he presumed, this said with an unkind sideways glance towards Fordham, after the birth of her baby. A suggested subscription of five shillings was settled, notwithstanding.

'Which brings us to the annual Recitation Prize competition,' George announced at length. 'Any questions?'

'Two,' Fordham said, while the rest summarily shook their heads. 'Has the Headmaster selected his candidate for the event? And is Heritage to judge it?'

'Patrick will indeed judge, Christopher, as he has always done, and my candidate will be Fergus Ash. Have any other candidates been put forward yet?' George inquired, and answered by an evasive silence, added, 'We do need some, you know. After all, this is a competition. All suggestions gratefully received, therefore.' He drove home the hint with an encouraging smile. 'Any other business?' Another silence followed. 'Meeting closed, then. Bertie?' he summoned, and with a formal nod to his staff led Braithwaite from the room.

Fordham waited for Dorothy to follow them, and remarked scornfully, 'So the Recitation Prize will be a charade as ever. George has selected the pious and deserving Ash, whom he will coach assiduously. A stooge or two will be wheeled on as token opposition and Patrick will then do his duty as tame judge. Result? Ash wins. The prize goes to the headmaster's candidate yet again.'

'Your objection is serious?' Gunz asked him.

'Absolutely.'

'Then why not do something about it?'

'Do something, Dr G.?' Fordham said in tones of mock amazement. 'Oh no, that's asking rather too much.'

'Then you don't mean what you say.'

'But I do.'

'Then you are evading the issue,' Gunz suggested impatiently.

'Dammit, Siggy,' Fordham snapped, 'Don't lecture me, I don't care for it. All I ask from life is a bit of fun and a bit of gin, and if you don't want Arabella, I've got a damn good mind to propose to her myself. She is at least prepared to provide both.'

'Good,' Gunz grunted. 'Do something about that, then.'

'Sorry, Siggy,' Fordham said a moment later, 'I didn't mean what I just said. Out of order. Forgive me.'

Gunz shrugged, and shaped a tolerant smile.

'But I did mean what I said about the competition,' Fordham insisted. 'I bet I could even tell you the passage George is going to select, if he hasn't already. It'll be something biblical, something we've heard before – George likes to repeat his successes.' He paused while a frown of concentration passed across his face, and then said confidently, 'Samuel Two, nineteen to twenty-seven, David's Lamentation. You know, "Lest the daughters of the Philistines rejoice".'

'Lest the daughters of the uncircumcised rejoice,' Gunz corrected him.

'That may well be deleted, Siggy.'

'Anyway, it's Samuel Two, nineteen to twenty-six.'

'Twenty-seven.'

'Twenty-six.'

'Half a crown?' Fordham suggested.

'You're on,' Gunz said with a grin, and rubbed his hands. 'Is there a Bible over there, Patrick?' he asked Heritage, who was hunched in a chair beneath a precipitously piled bookcase.

'Must be one here somewhere,' Heritage grumbled, and began to poke among the books that overhung him.

'I've made up my mind,' Fordham announced suddenly.

'I should hope so, Christopher,' Gunz advised. 'The bet is made.'

'No, I mean I'm going to come up with my own candidate.'

'Excellent,' said Gunz.

'Fancy a small bribe, Patrick?' Fordham asked, as Heritage tossed Gunz a battered Bible.

'I don't fancy the sack.'

Gunz riffled the Bible's pages briskly and pounced on one with a finger. 'Oh dear,' he declared disconsolately. 'Twenty-seven.'

'Half a crown, Dr G.,' Fordham reminded him, and then by way of explanation to Heritage, who had clearly missed the circumstances of the bet, he added,

'Nineteen to twenty-seven, Samuel Two, David's Lamentation.'

'Can't have it,' Heritage growled. 'George has already picked it for young Ash.'

'What did I say?' said Fordham smugly.

Gunz flipped the coin at him, and Fordham cupped it in his hand as it fell and pocketed it.

'Starting well on all fronts,' he observed.

Dorothy poked her head round the study door and said, 'Sir Foster's here. I've put him in the sitting room.'

'Well, Bertie?' George asked, when Dorothy had retreated into her office.

Braithwaite shot him a doubtful look.

'You're the one who normally comes up with the new ideas, aren't you? Fresh thinking, I admire you for it, you know.'

'Really?' Braithwaite said, brightening.

'I do think she will prove absolutely indispensable to the smooth running of the school, but the chairman is a little old-fashioned.'

'A little!'

'Very old-fashioned,' George conceded, adding, 'no bad thing, in many ways. The point I'm trying to make, Bertie, is that he could well attempt to scupper the whole thing on financial grounds, tell us we can't afford it.'

'I don't know that we can afford it, George.'

'And he'll use that as an excuse,' George continued quickly, 'to avoid facing up to the real issue, which is that he is resistant to the employment of what he sees as too many women in the school. Now you're a principled man, Bertie, I know that. We disagree over many things, but on this I know you and I are together.

A preparatory school needs women. You do agree?'

'Of course I agree, George, but – '

'Exactly,' George went on in the same cajoling tone, ignoring Braithwaite's intended protest. 'We've been fudging and making do for far too long. It's not fair on matron, it's not fair on Wendy. There's no getting away from it – we need a housekeeper.'

'Yes,' Braithwaite agreed hesitantly. 'It is, of course, a role commonly taken up by the headmaster's wife. I don't wish to pry, George, but . . .' He left the question unasked.

'I shall not be marrying Mrs Prior, Bertie, if that is what you wish to know. It is partly that which makes me realize that a housekeeper is now essential, whatever the cost, whatever the chairman's objections.'

'The extra salary does worry me.'

George rose from his desk. 'Bertie,' he said weightily. 'The principle of the thing is more important. I have to have your backing.'

Braithwaite held his expectant stare and said, 'We'll have to make some savings somewhere to pay for her.'

'Good man,' George said. 'We will.'

Sir Foster Gill greeted them a trifle huffily and declined George's offer of a sherry.

'No, no,' he insisted, 'here on business, so let's get on with it. Been doing a bit of thinking about your proposal, but as I told you, I'd value the bursar's view. The financial position. Just sounding a note of caution, George. Well, bursar?' he asked Braithwaite.

'The fact of the matter is, Sir Foster, we've trundled along here rather rudderless on the domestic side. There's matron, of course, and her girls, and Dorothy and George too, and myself, yes, and we've made a pretty good fist of catering, dormitory planning, domestic staff supervision, all the homely arrangements.' He cleared his throat slightly and glanced at George. 'But in the modern school one needs more,' he declared. 'The school needs more.'

'I absolutely agree,' Gill said without hesitation. 'I approve of a housekeeper. But in our present financial position won't she be something of a luxury?'

'I believe we could afford the extra salary,' George said firmly.

'Bursar?'

'It is, I believe, a matter of principle, Sir Foster,' Braithwaite told him sternly.

'Is it? Principle?' Each eager question was accompanied by a pecking motion of the head, which his bird-like features made appear entirely natural. 'Oh, well, then,' he went on, 'that's settled. I just wasn't sure about the cash. Set the wheels in motion.'

'Thank you, chairman,' George beamed.

'I think I will have that sherry after all, George,' Gill said, and while George was at the sideboard, turned to Braithwaite and inquired, 'Busy, Braithwaite? Don't let me keep you.'

Braithwaite got up.

'I am, Sir Foster,' he agreed. 'Always busy.'

'Good, good,' Gill observed vaguely.

'I'll look in later, George,' Braithwaite suggested, as George returned with Gill's glass. 'Discuss the details.'

'Yes, thanks, Bertie.'

'Good man, Braithwaite,' Gill remarked, when he had gone. 'Technical. Gunner. Never thought he was quite HQ.' He sniffed his sherry. 'You're up to something, George.'

'Chairman?'

'Don't play the innocent with me,' Gill growled.

'What happened to that awfully nice widow you were so fond of?'

'Sadly, nothing.'

'Not for me to comment,' Gill said. 'Pity, though. She could have taken on a duty or two. Wouldn't need a housekeeper then, would we?'

'I think it's asking rather a lot of a woman to expect her to take on a place like this – in addition to a husband.'

'Was that what she jibbed at?' Gill asked, his eyes narrowing in disbelief. 'This place?' When George made no comment, he said, 'Better find the right housekeeper then, hadn't you? Might make a difference to your Mrs Prior.' He shot George a sudden beaky stare. 'Hadn't thought of that, had you?' he inquired, but George looked back obliquely. 'No. Good luck, though. I support you. God knows how you talked Braithwaite round.'

George appeared to be wholly occupied in peering at the glass between Gill's fingers.

'Ready for another one, Sir Foster?'

'The deed is done,' Fordham announced, having dumped a pile of books untidily on the table. 'The die is cast. The course is set.'

Heritage eyed him crossly from behind a stack of exercise books, and Gunz's spectacles glinted in the orange glow of the wireless dial, as he too gave him an inquiring glance.

'Phillips,' Fordham said in the same declamatory tone.

'What about Phillips?' Heritage asked with evident disapproval.

'What do you think of him?'

'He's appalling, that's what I think of him.'

'Phillips of the libellous skit?' Gunz asked.

'The very same.'

'Patrick's right,' Gunz said, turning back to the wireless. 'He is appalling.'

'But talented,' Fordham protested.

'Undeniably talented,' Gunz agreed, 'but nevertheless appalling.' He thumped the top of the set. 'Not only can I not get Vienna on this machine,' he complained, 'I cannot even get Hamburg.'

'He's my candidate,' Fordham said, 'for the Recitation Prize. The boy's morals are one thing, his abilities quite another. I foresee a future for him on the stage. He has presence. He is compelling.'

Gunz clicked off the radio.

'Surely you are not serious, Christopher.'

'I am entirely serious.'

'If I may say so,' Heritage observed unhappily, 'this will cause the gravest offence.'

'Nonsense, Patrick,' Fordham said, grinning.

Heritage put down his pen and leaned on the pile of books.

'Phillips has behaved extremely badly this term,' he said, 'and by and large he's got away with it. He writes a scurrilous lampoon, mocking each and every one of us, and because he's got so near the knuckle, we have to pretend we don't know anything about it. I agree that the boy has spirit, but to put him up for a prize is to indicate that we approve of his activities.'

'I don't see that at all.'

'Well, I do.'

'Dammit, Patrick, you're the judge!' Fordham retorted angrily. 'You're supposed to be objective.'

'I am objective.'

'No, you're not, you've just said as much.'

'A neutral attitude towards Phillips is fine,' Heritage conceded. 'But as for larding him with glory!'

'He will be so good,' Fordham warned, 'that he will have to win the prize – and the glory too.'

Heritage grunted and flipped open an exercise book.

'What piece have you chosen for Phillips to recite, Christopher?' Gunz asked.

'"Rock Around the Clock",' Heritage muttered into his book. 'By that appropriately up-to-the-minute poet, Mr William Haley. Accompanied, no doubt, by Jones and Parker on the kazoo and washboard.'

'I will offer, or rather Phillips will offer,' Fordham said, ignoring the jibe '"The Badger".'

'I don't know it,' said Gunz.

'You don't listen to rock'n'roll,' Heritage grumbled.

'It is not rock'n'roll,' Fordham said flatly. 'It is from the Middle Ages, an Old English riddle in the Exeter Book. "White is my neck, head yellow, sides the same" – and so on and so forth. It is quite remarkably fine and Phillips will be quite remarkably good. All we require is an unbiased judge.' He glared at Heritage, who remained pointedly busy with his books; Gunz turned the wireless on again. 'All I want to do is give George a run for his money,' he groaned, but got no answer.

'Well, damn it,' he said defiantly, 'I'm not changing my mind for either of you.'

'Ah!' Gunz explained in a triumphant tone at the same instant. 'I think I have something.'

But what ricocheted unexpectedly off the airwaves came from nowhere so civilized as the capitals of Europe: a hideous caterwauling, unintelligible, yet at once menacing and lascivious, accompanied by a piano whose keys were apparently pounded by a roadmender's drill, the whole pagan incantation borne along on a jolting beat every bit as primitive and dangerous as jungle drums.

Gunz and Heritage stared at one another aghast, their heads shaking slowly in the way of old men faced with the folly of youth.

George was inspecting his appearance critically in the hall mirror, tweaking a jowl experimentally between thumb and forefinger, when Charles bounded downstairs and said, 'Oh good, I'm not late.' He took his father's place at the mirror, surveying his reflection with an unmistakable air of satisfaction that George found irritating. 'No one here yet?' he asked.

George looked at his watch.

'The only way I could get my staff here a moment before the appointed hour would be to start serving gin instead of my second-best sherry,' he observed drily. 'And that being the case, they would undoubtedly polish off so much of the stuff that we wouldn't be able to afford a housekeeper. What do you think of her?'

Charles shrugged. 'I haven't had time to form an opinion. Why?'

George stuffed his hands in his pockets and frowned. 'Cold feet,' he explained. 'Even Bertie spotted it – there's something odd about her. She was evasive about her last employer for one thing. I don't know, nothing to put one's finger on.'

'Why go for her if you've got doubts?'

'No alternative. We saw a procession of stout elderly women with bees in their bonnets about virtually everything – made matron seem a positive treasure.' A laugh exploded from Charles at this remark, but George assured him, 'Believe me, Charles, they were dreadful. And there was only one other younger woman, who appeared to be on the verge of bursting into tears. Nice, but I couldn't risk her. Which left Mrs Stephenson.'

'Or another advert. Or, indeed, no housekeeper at all.' Charles paused, then continued teasingly, 'I am forced to the reluctant conclusion that my esteemed papa has been pushing things a little.'

'I have,' George admitted, 'and I wouldn't admit this to anyone else, anyone, so don't you breathe a word. I have been behaving quite badly of late, and do you know, I find it quite invigorating? I want Mary. I want Drummonds. But I want Mary enough to run the risk of, well, problems at the school.'

'Will she be a risk?'

'Mrs Stephenson? Certainly. I don't know enough about the woman,' George declared airily. 'But I want to show Mary that she can marry me without having to marry Drummonds. She can be my wife and leave here every morning and spend the day employed in Bennett's antique business. All I want is her presence in the evenings – and at night. I'm not so stupid as to believe that hiring a housekeeper will make any profound difference to her, but it will at least destroy one excuse.. She can't deny me on those grounds any more. She's going to have to make up her own mind about me as I am. Drummonds doesn't come into it any more.' Interrupted by the doorbell, he added, 'All I need is for Mrs Stephenson to last long enough for me to get my argument across to Mary.'

As he went to open the door, he turned to Charles and said, 'Look, I'm not going to be able to do this every time someone arrives, so would you mind letting people in? Just hover somewhere handy. And keep Mary out here when she turns up. I want to have a quiet word before she gets swallowed up by the crowd.'

*

In the event George's 'quiet word' was abridged to the briefest of explanations for her invitation while he helped Mary off with her coat, and it wasn't until the gathering began to thin out that they found themselves sufficiently alone for her to tell him, 'I'm still trying to work out why you asked me to come.'

'To meet Mrs Stephenson. I told you.'

'I was expecting someone round and fat and dumpy – not a rival,' Mary remarked lightly.

'She isn't,' George said. 'I rang you the other day and a man answered. It threw me a little. I put the phone down.'

'So it was you, George. I did wonder.'

'Who was he?'

While Mary hesitated, Dorothy homed in on them and gushed, 'Just wanted to say, I think she's quite lovely.' And as she drifted off, Mary spotted Sir Foster Gill edging towards them.

'We can't talk here,' she said, giving George a warning nudge.

He read her signal and said, 'No,' then added in an urgent whisper, 'Give me half an hour and they'll all be gone.'

It was almost an hour before George saw the stragglers out, and he leaned against the front door after he had closed it for the last time and let out a long breath.

'Quite a success,' Mary observed.

'The soireé? Or Mrs Stephenson?'

'Both,' said Mary. 'Dorothy's right – she is lovely. Where's Charles?'

'He escaped some time ago. Unless you're intending to talk into the early hours, I don't think you need worry about him disturbing us. Come on,' he said, taking Mary's hand and leading her back into the sitting room. 'I feel as if I haven't sat down for a week.'

As soon as he was stretched out in his armchair, he said, 'I'd better come clean. By employing Audrey, I'm making it clear that no one will ever come to you with crises over tuck or re-ordering bed linen or "Can I have an extra day at home at half term because Daddy's on leave from Cyprus?" You won't need to take on the school – just me.'

'Did you really think it out that clearly, George?' Mary asked, astonished and amused.

'I'm ashamed to say I did,' he admitted, but after a moment's reflection and in an altogether more positive tone, he said, 'In fact I'm not ashamed at all. I'm really feeling rather smug.'

'Good for you.'

George uttered an abrupt laugh. 'But is it?' he asked her. 'Good for me? A display of pure selfishness? A man out for number one?'

'It's very good for you,' Mary replied. 'You've spent your whole life being reasonable and thinking of others, and now at long last you're thinking of yourself.'

'Yes,' George said hesitantly. 'I still find it difficult to see that as an advance. If the whole world behaved like that!'

'Who cares about the whole world?' Mary demanded, restless with exasperation. 'The whole world can go hang. Everybody has to accommodate a little, of course, but you can accommodate too much, George. Even now you're claiming that all this is selfishness on your part, when it's nothing of the sort. It's giving in to me, letting me have my own way, isn't it?'

'I don't see it like that.'

'There are times,' Mary said, with a hard look, 'when you can be the most dreadful prig.'

'Really?' George snapped, piqued by her remark. 'Hardly any wonder you don't want to marry me then. I didn't see it as giving in to you. I thought your doubts entirely sensible, the natural worries of a mature woman. I hadn't realized that it was all some sort of ploy – a game.' A sulky silence set in, which George interrupted by saying, 'The fellow who answered the phone – '

'This has nothing to do with James.'

'Oh, no?'

'No. I might just as well question you about Audrey. After all, I understand why you want to employ a housekeeper, fine. But this particular housekeeper?'

George raised his hands in a gesture of apology, which he reinforced with a smile. 'All right,' he said, 'no more jumping to conclusions. Actually, Audrey's appointment does worry me more than I care to admit. Is she a wrong 'un, eh?' he drawled in an exaggerated rustic twang.

'Surely not,' Mary said, and glanced at her watch. 'I'd better go.'

Instead of getting up, George seemed to sag in his seat.

'I haven't responded properly, have I, George?'

'You've responded truthfully,' George sighed. 'You always do.'

'I don't know what to think,' Mary said wearily.

'No,' said George, but then he brightened. 'Why don't you come up to the school next week and do a bit of surreptitious spying for me? On la Stephenson.'

'Why me?' Mary protested gently.

'Who else is going to tell me what they think?

Dorothy defends all my decisions, willy-nilly. Bertie's lumbered. I need you.'

'We'll see,' Mary murmured.

'I hope so.'

14

Practice had turned morning and bed-time in the baby dorm into a brisk routine of dressing and undressing, face flannelling, the brushing of teeth and hair, and the saying of prayers, complicated from day to day by baths and by the periodic changing of bed linen and, at different intervals, of various articles of clothing, and by inspections for cleanliness of certain items.

'Right,' said Wendy, walking in. 'Shoes.' She clapped her hands twice to instil a sense of urgency. 'Come on, you've had plenty of time.'

The drill was to stand in line with a hand stuck in each polished shoe, so that the pair could be turned under Wendy's eyes as she passed.

'Good,' she said repeatedly until she came to Brown and Prior, when she stopped and shook her head. 'Right,' she said, turning to the others, 'you can carry on, but as for you two,' she continued, confronting Brown and Prior, 'it's just not good enough. Those shoes haven't seen a smudge of polish between them. What's your excuse?'

'Forgot, sir,' Brown said sheepishly.

'But Wednesday night is always shoe night, isn't it?'

'Yes, sir,' said Prior, staring sadly at his shabby footwear.

'Very well,' Wendy went on. 'I'm going to put a note in my diary. I want to see you both in my room a week from today, and I want you to bring everyone's shoes, every pair in this dormitory, and you two will have cleaned the lot. Do you understand?'

'But, sir – '

'No buts, Brown. Next Wednesday. I'll make a note in my diary right now, so don't think I'm going to forget.'

'Good night, everybody!' George called from the doorway, but catching the end of Wendy's warning, came over.

'Look at these, Headmaster,' Wendy said severely, indicating the unpolished shoes.

George shook his head, tutting, and said, 'Quite dreadful.' Then he patted Brown on the head, and added, 'I'm sure Wendy has an appropriate punishment in mind.' He turned to Prior, but hesitated, and thrust his hands stiffly behind his back. 'Good night now,' he told them both.

'Good night, sir,' they replied.

'Next Wednesday, mind,' Wendy reminded them. 'Now, get ready for prayers.'

'He likes you,' Prior whispered to Brown across his shoulder, as he knelt beside his bed.

'Who likes me?' Brown whispered back.

'Mr Drummond. But I don't think he likes me.'

When she heard the knock at her door, Wendy stayed where she sat on her bed, massaging the soles of sore feet between her palms. But she said hullo in answer, and looked up as Charles came in carrying two bottles of beer.

'I thought you'd be back by now,' he said. 'D'you fancy one?'

Wendy nodded, and he levered the tops off with an opener he fished from his pocket, took two glasses from the glass shelf above the basin and filled them carefully.

'Oh, come on, Wendy,' he said, handing one to her. 'What's it all about? The new outfit. The afternoon off. I saw you when I was on my way back from cross country – you looked absolutely stunning. So come on, where were you off to?'

'I went for an interview.'

'For a job?'

Wendy nodded, and sipped her beer silently.

'But I thought dad had just given you some extra responsibilities?'

'He has – and I appreciate it,' she added quickly, 'but the occasional class of conversational French doesn't exactly open unlimited horizons.'

Charles grinned. 'I didn't even know you spoke French.'

'No, you didn't, did you?' Wendy observed coolly.

'My fault for not finding out, I suppose.'

'I'm not that good anyway.'

'So what was the job you went for?' Charles asked.

'Secretary to the secretary of a golf club – quite a classy one.'

'But you don't type.'

'Wrong again, Charles. And I do shorthand.'

'How did you get on?' There was a note of uncertainty in Charles' question.

'Very well, I think,' Wendy said. 'The pay's not much, so I don't imagine there'll be that much competition.'

'Hell, Wendy,' Charles muttered, 'this isn't a lot of fun.'

'And my uncle knows one of the men on the committee, which obviously helps,' Wendy went on breezily. 'I should know by the weekend.'

'You mean you'll take it?' Charles demanded urgently.

'I did apply for it, Charles.'

'Does dad know?'

'I think he has an idea.'

'Well, he might have said something to me! Hell, Wendy!' he said, and sucked angrily at his beer.

'Of course, I'll miss it here.'

'Oh, will you?' Charles snapped.

'Yes,' Wendy replied evenly. 'And I'll miss your father, and you too, and Susan, and Dorothy.'

'And just about everybody, I suppose,' Charles sneered, then he asked sharply, 'It's nothing to do with Mrs Stephenson, is it?'

'Of course not.'

'If matron were to be believed, she's got the entire domestic staff of the school up in arms.'

'I think she's a charming woman, and certainly efficient.' Wendy held his eyes and said, 'No, Charles, I just need a change.'

Charles slid on to the bed beside her and slipped his arm behind her back. 'You're not really serious, are you?' he murmured into her ear.

Wendy wriggled away and stood up. 'Don't be pathetic,' she said impatiently.

Charles glowered at her, but then grinned. 'Serves us all right, I suppose,' he observed. 'Or serves me right, I should say.' He shrugged. 'Want some more?'

Wendy held out her glass.

'I don't want you to go,' Charles said as he took it. 'I don't want you to go at all.' But Wendy looked away from his sad eyes.

'Are you sure it's all right to wait in here?' Mary asked, hesitating in the doorway as Dorothy showed her into George's study.

'Of course it is,' Dorothy insisted, and nudged her into the room. 'He'll be delighted to see you, I'm sure. He's just a bit stuck with some parents. A fearfully dim child, and they simply cannot understand why he's not winning scholarships to Winchester and suchlike. He'll be pleased as punch to see you after them.'

'By contrast, you mean?' Mary inquired.

'Go away with you,' Dorothy protested. 'That's not what I meant at all. What brought you up here anyway?'

'I was just passing, and I want to see if I can have Edward at home next weekend. My mother's coming down and she'll want to see him.'

'Oh, that won't be a bother,' Dorothy assured her. 'Happens all the time. But I'd better not let the head catch me gassing,' she added, making for the door.

'How's Mrs Stephenson settling in?' Mary asked hurriedly, and Dorothy stopped and turned.

'I wish I knew, dear,' she said. 'They tell me the Sphinx is female – probably modelled on her. I can't be doing with it. Too mysterious for words.'

'She struck me as very pleasant.'

'I couldn't hear a word against her,' Dorothy agreed. 'The men, of course, are buzzing like bees round a honey-pot. But the thing is, she's a bit toffee-nosed, and no one can quite work out why she's here.' She dropped her voice and went on, mock mysteriously, 'What, we ask, went on at Lord Tiddleypush's to make her want to leave?'

While her question hung archly in the air, George burst in.

'Mary!' he exclaimed happily.

'I hope I'm all right in here, George,' Mary said. 'Dorothy told me you were busy.'

'Yes,' George replied. 'Parents should be abolished.'

'I'll go this instant.'

'You don't count,' George beamed. 'You'll stay and have – what would you like to have?'

'Nothing.'

'Nothing?' Dorothy echoed.

'Nothing. Really. Thank you.'

There was a pause after Dorothy closed the door, and then George said, 'Want to see the plans? For the music school?' He pointed at the plans, which were spread across his desk, went over to them and shook his head. 'Sheer bloody fantasy, if you ask me,' he grumbled. 'Quite out of keeping. I've told Brown too. This is a small, quiet, rural backwater. If we are to have a music school, it has to be something appropriate. But as Brown's paying, I suppose he thinks he can call the tune.'

'They're like something the mekon might have designed,' Mary observed with a frown, adding, 'Edward's indoctrinated me into the world of Dan Dare.'

George's expression lightened momentarily, then darkened again. 'It's neo-modernism, or so I'm informed,' he explained gloomily. 'Looks like a pill box with wings, if you ask me. I can't accept it, can I? Or am I just being reactionary old George?'

'If you are, I approve.'

George lifted a book which was placed squarely on one side of the plans, and the edge lifted and curled, rolling across the desk to form a fat tube; he took a paperweight from the opposite edge, picked up the roll of paper, and dropped it into a waste basket behind his desk. As he did so, he said, 'You do? Right, I'll ring Brown in the morning.' Then he looked at Mary. 'Hullo.'

'Hullo.'

To escape the silence that followed, Mary said, 'I

wanted to ask you if I could have Edward home at the weekend.'

'Of course.'

'My mother's coming.'

'Good.'

'He won't be wanted for a vital match or anything?'

'If he is, I'm sure his grandmother is more important.'

The same silence settled on them again, and Mary moved to the window. 'The crocuses are showing,' she remarked.

'Spring on its way.'

Mary turned, and they caught each other's eyes.

'I was just going to say . . .' Mary began, but hesitated, and continued quickly, 'Those plans really are awful, aren't they? Look, I'd better dash. Bye, George, and thank you.'

She was leaving as she spoke, grabbing her bag from the chair where she had dropped it and darting into Dorothy's office without a backward glance.

'Goodbye,' George said to the door, as Mary pulled it shut behind her.

The packed hall was silent except for the high, clear voice of Fergus Ash, which rang out thrillingly from the stage. His stance was straight, his shoulders square, his head tilted slightly back so that his glasses glinted under the lights. Behind them his eyes burned with a biblical fire, while the mouth below his sharp nose shaped every syllable precisely.

'How are the mighty fallen,' he cried one last time, 'and the weapons of war perished!'

As the final consonant cracked across the heads of his audience, Ash bent into a deep bow from which a roar of applause jerked him upright again, his face taut with emotion. Then he marched to the side of the stage and sat down, Phillips rising simultaneously from the seat beside him.

In contrast to Ash's soldierish stance, Phillips adopted a position that was almost a crouch, and as his voice began to rise and fall with the rhythm of his lines, his eyes wandered the audience with a discomfiting predatory glint which even flashed across the faces of his headmaster and Heritage, who looked down to scribble in a notebook. At times his voice dropped to a shrill whisper, but as he approached the climax of his monologue, his throat throbbed with a menacing growl that seemed not to belong to the boy: 'I shall turn and attack and shall viciously spear, this creature I hate who has harried me there!'

The entire audience stared at him, entranced by his powerful oration, but then, as Fordham began to applaud loudly, the hall erupted in thunderous approval, which was not silenced until Heritage rose from the front row, clambered on to the stage, and held up his hand.

'Now, now, what a task, eh?' He nodded towards the row of anxious competitors, and continued, 'This year's finalists for the Drummonds School Recitation Prize have achieved an exceptionally high standard, I think you'll all agree. They've obviously worked very hard, every one of them, and if it hasn't been easy for them, well, I can tell you it hasn't been easy for me either. But I've come to a decision, and if anyone accuses me of being biased, then all I can say is I've honestly tried not to be. But as you all know, I am also a scoutmaster, and perhaps because of that I was particularly moved by one piece. It was also quite beautifully spoken.'

Turning to the side of the stage, he tucked his

notebook under his arm, and announced, 'The prize goes to Michael Phillips for "The Badger".' And he led renewed applause as Phillips, grinning delightedly, stepped to the centre of the stage.

Fordham caught Gunz's eye above the cheering crowd and winked, then turned to find George in front of him.

'I don't mind having lost against such a splendid performance,' George said warmly, pumping Fordham's hand. 'A particularly imaginative choice of subject. Well done, Christopher.'

Fordham, his face already flushed with triumph, responded with a grin as broad as his candidate's.

'Thank you, Headmaster, thank you.'

'Hello, Wendy,' Mary said from the doorway of the baby dorm. 'Seen Edward?'

Wendy turned round and dropped a fold of sheet which had been clamped between her chin and her chest.

'Oh, Mrs Prior, good morning,' she answered, trying to retrieve the lost fold without a free hand. 'No, I'm afraid not. Hang on though,' she said, and called, 'Christie!' to a boy she saw in the corridor. Mary stood aside to let him in, and Wendy told him, 'Go and see if you can find Prior, Christie. His mother's come to collect him for the weekend. Quick as you can.'

As the boy scampered out, Mary strolled across to her son's bed and sat down.

'Not in your way, am I?' she asked.

'No, it's nice to have someone to talk to.'

At that moment George came in.

'I heard you were here,' he said. 'A search is going on for Edward.'

'Hello, George.'

'Has Wendy told you her news?' he asked. 'She's leaving us.'

'No, Wendy!' Mary exclaimed, surprised.

'I got an offer this morning,' Wendy explained almost awkwardly. 'Job at a golf club.'

'What a pity,' Mary said, then added, 'I'm sorry, I shouldn't say that, should I?'

'Yes, you should,' George said. 'I'm trying to find ways of persuading her to stay. Not very successful though, am I, Wendy? And the worst of it is I rather understand,' he sighed.

'Don't,' Wendy told him. 'Please.'

She left the room with an armful of dirty linen, and George said, 'Thank you for that snap reaction, Mary. I wish I could make her stay. Now, do you want me to go in search of your errant offspring?'

'I'd better wait here,' Mary suggested. 'If I move we'll never find each other.'

'Siggy thinks he has the makings of a scientist,' George remarked. 'An inquiring mind.'

'And what do you think, George?'

'About Edward?' he asked, and shrugged.

'I haven't managed any spying for you, I'm afraid,' Mary said, and seeing George's bemused look, explained, 'on Mrs Stephenson.'

'Ah,' George said noncommittally, provoking an awkward silence which was broken by matron's brusque and unexpected entry.

'Headmaster, there you are,' she declared in a tone that implied he ought to have been somewhere else. 'And Mrs Prior. My God, what's happening in here?' she demanded, glaring at the unmade beds. 'Where are the sheets? It's got to stop. Enough is enough, Headmaster. All my household duties gone! What's left – aspirin and sticking plasters?'

Having eyed her with increasing irritation during this outburst, George said, 'What exactly are you talking about, matron?'

'First I discover from the bursar that she has made alternative arrangements not only for the laundry, but also the mending service, without so much as a word of consultation, mind, and when I point out to her politely that she has overstepped her duties, she tells me to shut up and insults me in front of a fellow member of staff.'

'I take it you are referring to Mrs Stephenson?' George inquired.

'She's got to go,' matron told him flatly.

'I don't agree, matron.'

'No?' she snapped. 'Well, let me tell you, unless she's prepared to make a formal apology . . .'

The threat remained unformed.

'Yes?' George prompted her.

'I cannot tell you your job, Headmaster –'

'Indeed not,' George warned her.

'But I have to say,' she went on, 'that in this instance your choice was most unfortunate.'

'Indeed?' George remarked coldly. 'And tell me, matron, do you think Mrs Stephenson is likely to make you a formal apology?'

'If instructed to by you.'

'And if I have no intention of issuing such an instruction? What then?'

Matron flicked an invisible speck from her bib and cleared her throat.

'Then I will be unable to work with the woman,' she said unsteadily. 'She will have to go.'

'Understand me, matron,' George advised. 'Whether or not Mrs Stephenson stays or goes or apologizes, or dresses up like a Christmas tree fairy, I make the decision, not you.'

'I see, I see,' matron agreed uneasily.

'And as far as I am concerned,' George continued, 'my choice of Mrs Stephenson has so far proved entirely correct. She is doing her job not merely well, excellently well, but furthermore, exactly as I would wish her to do it. My message to you therefore, matron, to put it bluntly, is like it or lump it.'

'I will not be spoken to like that, Mr Drummond, not by you or anybody,' matron protested.

'I apologize for my tone,' George said, 'but the message remains the same.'

'Well! Well!' matron retorted huffily.

'And since you find yourself in an untenable situation, I will accept a week's notice – or a month, if you prefer.'

'Then you shall have it, Mr Drummond,' she declared. 'Good day to you.'

Her rubber soles squealed noisily on the wooden floor, as she hurried from the dormitory. George rubbed his face fiercely.

'Bloody woman!' he muttered. 'Plays no part in the life of the school, hides away in her room all day long, and only comes out to cause trouble. We're well shot of her.'

'You must think very highly of Mrs Stephenson,' Mary observed.

George closed his eyes and drew in a deep breath; when he opened his eyes, he looked hard at Mary.

'I can't live on this emotional switchback any longer,' he told her. 'My work's suffering and my life is suffering. I'd be grateful if you kept as well clear of the school as possible from now on.'

'But why, George?' Mary asked, shocked.

'Because, damn it, I wish it that way. I can't take all

this drama. You keep turning up here with your chummy "Hello, George, let's be just good friends", and I've realized I'm not capable of being just good friends with you. I'd rather you went away now, and stayed away. And I have to say this, I'd rather you took Edward away from school at the end of term.'

Mary's face dropped and she stared at George aghast.

'I can't bear to see him,' he continued, shaking his head wretchedly. 'Every time I see him, I think of you. I see you in his face, his smile, his eyes – and I can't take it. I can't talk to him, I can't treat him like the other boys, I'm no good as his headmaster, and he'd be far better off at another school. We've got to cut ourselves apart, Mary, now and forever.'

George turned and walked wearily away, leaving Mary slumped in silent shock on Edward's bed.

She had not moved when, several minutes later, Edward raced into the room and bounced on to the bed beside her. She pulled him tightly to her, but he broke away, bobbing excitedly on his knees.

'Mummy, there's a real rugby match next week against another school, and I'm playing.' He hesitated, his hand hovering in front of his mouth, then he went on, 'I think it's called wing – because I'm a good runner.'

'I think I must be mad,' Mary murmured, not hearing him.

'I said if I'm wing I ought to fly, not run,' Edward giggled. 'It's a joke,' he explained, looking disappointed at his mother.

'What darling?' she asked vaguely.

'A joke,' he sighed.

*

'I'll go and find Wendy this very minute, father,' Charles said, clearly too excited to remain in the room any longer. 'I can't see how she could turn it down.' A look of concern shadowed his face abruptly, and he asked anxiously, 'Are you all right?'

'I shall be,' George replied.

Charles hung to the edge of the door for a moment, then flashed a parting grin, and ducked from view, his place in the doorway being taken by Dorothy.

'What now, Dorothy?' he groaned. 'Not another resignation, I hope.'

'Mrs Prior,' she said, and closed the door quietly as soon as Mary had slipped past her.

'I meant it, Mary,' George said from behind his desk.

'I know you meant it,' Mary said so softly that George strained to hear her.

'There's no alternative.'

'Isn't there?' she asked, while a point of light danced in each eye.